MISADVENTURES

WITH

MY EX

BY
SHAYLA BLACK

MISADVENTURES

WITH

MY EX

BY
SHAYLA BLACK

WATERHOUSE PRESS

*To everyone who had a second chance
and found love.*

CHAPTER ONE

WEST

Los Angeles
October

"If that son of a bitch hadn't given in to his case of cold feet, I would be on a beach somewhere—like Bora Bora or Bali or Barbados. Why do all the best beaches start with a B?"

As I look through the small, airy apartment, I can't see the woman who slurs the words, but I'd know Eryn Hope's voice anywhere.

"I would be soaking up the sun, enjoying my life, and glowing from multiple orgasms because, even though Weston Quaid is a total bastard, he was always amazing in bed."

My former fiancée's younger sister, Echo, stands in the open door, wincing. "You didn't hear that."

Though I'd rather not be here, and I probably should have come equipped with a steel-girded jockstrap and a shield to protect myself from what I suspect will be a shit fight, I can't not grin. "Not a word."

"But *nooo*. I'm getting romantic with Ernest and Julio Gallo. They don't give orgasms." Eryn huffs. "Hey, if that was the pizza guy who rang the doorbell, bring me a slice, will you? I need something to soak up this merlot."

"Eryn is just...having a bad day," Echo murmurs.

Because life in general has been rough or because, if things had ended differently, my former fiancée and I would be celebrating our third wedding anniversary tonight?

"I understand."

Truthfully, today has sucked for me, too. I've avoided thinking about the significance of this date since I woke up. Too many what-ifs and memories. Since I walked away from Eryn, I've fought a gritty, ugly uphill battle. It's almost over. I seem to be winning now...but along the way, I've taken terrible losses.

"Maybe you should go." Echo begins to close the door. "She's not exactly sober."

I wedge my foot past the threshold. "Waiting isn't an option. I need to see your sister tonight. It's business."

Echo frowns. "What business could you two possibly have? Eryn won't want to see you now. Maybe not ever."

I'm not surprised. Or deterred. "I—"

"Pizza?" A teenage kid wearing a collared shirt with a well-known chain's logo dashes up the stairs, an insulated carrier balanced on his palm.

I take out my wallet and pay the guy, tipping handsomely so this interruption will go away.

"Thanks!" the high schooler calls over his shoulder as he runs back down the steps.

"You didn't have to do that," Echo insists, cash in hand.

"I'd like to deliver this to your sister personally. Alone."

Echo hesitates. She's usually free-spirited, funny, and easy-breezy. Once, we shared a good camaraderie. Not surprisingly, that's gone. Hell, I'm shocked she's speaking to me at all.

As usual, she's dressed as if she belongs in a granola commercial. Today, it's braids and flannel, cargo shorts, knee socks, and hiking boots. She's an original. But she's also fiercely protective of both her older sisters, just as they're protective of her.

"I don't know if she can handle that," Eryn's sister admits. "To be honest, this day is rough on her every year."

I've come to dread October fourth, too. My younger brother, Flynn, pointed out this morning that the first year after my split with Eryn wrecked me, but he's relieved I got over her.

Clearly, I have him fooled.

But I'm not here to win Eryn back. And after the way our split went down, I'm sure that's impossible.

"Your sister bought a restaurant recently. I need to talk to her about it. Only talk," I assure Echo. "I'll make sure she gets fed, sobered up, and safely in bed. No fighting. Just conversation. I'll keep my hands to myself." *Even if I'm dying to touch her.*

"Echo, where's the damn pizza?" Eryn calls again from somewhere deeper in her apartment. "If I have to eat mediocre pie instead of fresh seafood on the freaking beach in the Bahamas—see, another great beach that starts with a B—I'd like it hot."

"Coming." But Echo doesn't move, simply blinks at me.

Is she surprised I know about Eryn's new endeavor? Gauging my sincerity? Probably both.

"Echo, I wouldn't ask to see her, especially tonight, if it wasn't important."

Finally, she sighs and lets me inside. "All right. Only because I don't think she'll ever move on until you two have talked."

Guilt stings. I handled our breakup horribly. True, I'd been blindsided and was reeling myself. I've been over those dark days in my head a thousand times. I can't change how everything unfolded now, and I didn't come here to rehash the past, but maybe while I handle business I can give her some peace.

"Thank you."

Echo lingers. "So, you're a bigwig CEO now?"

I can't miss her subtle dig. "Yes."

"Congratulations...I guess."

She's judging me for seemingly prioritizing business above love. I get it. That's not exactly true, but I understand it must appear that way. At the time, I made the only choice I thought I could. Only distance and perspective have made me second-guess that.

"How's school?" I change the subject. "You're close to finishing, right?"

"I graduate in May, then after my internship I'll be adulting full-time." Her grim smile melts into a frown. "Be good to my sister. Don't make me regret showing you mercy. Tell her I'll call her tomorrow."

"Of course."

Without another word, she grabs her overstuffed wallet, knit ski cap, and giant chain of dangling key rings, then nods as she closes the door behind her with a quiet snick.

After three long years, I'm alone with Eryn Hope. Maybe I'll have the chance to apologize for what I can't control now... and what I didn't know how to stop then. She might understand. But I'm realistic. This is Eryn. Thanks to a chaotic childhood with workaholic parents, she was cynical even before we met. I can only imagine how guarded she'll be now.

After all, I left her on our wedding day.

I step past the stylishly lived-in kitchen and deeper into the apartment that has a vintage, Audrey Hepburnesque vibe. It's so Eryn. My heart thumps madly the closer I come to her. Not surprising. After all, losing her was the worst mistake I ever made. Not a day goes by that I don't think of her.

"What's taking so long?" she calls. From the bedroom, maybe?

She's moved since our engagement. We both have. The apartment we shared here in LA was probably too full of ghosts and memories for her to remain. And after more than two years in New York, I've now settled in Las Vegas.

"Echo, you're listening, right? I'm pouring my heart out," Eryn continues with a sigh. "You know what sucks more? It's like that bastard ruined me. I can't orgasm with anyone else. And—oh, god—I still masturbate to thoughts of him. What's wrong with me?"

It might make me an asshole, but I don't hate knowing that no one else has pleased Eryn's sweet, petite curves as well as I did. In fact, I swell with more than masculine pride when I remember all the ways I once wrung screams from her.

I wish I could have even one night with my ex again.

On soft footfalls, I cross the kitschy-chic black-and-white living room, then find the bedroom tucked away through an alcove on the right. I lean against the doorframe, shoulder braced, and watch as my deepest regret paces the small bedroom in bare feet—and adorned in the wedding dress I never had the pleasure of seeing her wear.

I wish like hell we'd made it to the altar so I'd have the right to put my arms around her, kiss her neck, and seduce her straight into bed. Logically, I know the smartest course of action now would be to give her the unfortunate news about the property that houses her restaurant, then maybe broach an honest conversation about our past before I leave her in peace. Maybe afterward we'd both be able to heal and be happy.

Because the woman in front of me clearly isn't. And for that, I'm beyond sorry.

"There's nothing wrong with you, honey," I tell her. "I still think of you, too. All the time."

Eryn whirls with a gasp, a nearly empty bottle of red wine in hand. "West?"

When our stares meet, it's a sucker punch to my solar plexus. I stare at her haunting dark eyes in her shocked pale face. She blinks. Her rosy lips part as if she means to speak, but she doesn't say another word.

My former fiancée is even more beautiful than before. How is that possible?

"Hi," I say, my voice rough.

"This can't be happening. I haven't seen you in three

years, and now I'm suddenly seeing two of you?" She shakes her head. "No. You're a hallucination. You'll go away."

Repressing a smile, I set the warm pizza box on her rumpled bed, trying not to notice that the sheets smell like Eryn. Baby powder and vanilla and something musky that always turned me on. I've never experienced a similar fragrance on any other woman. I can't identify it, but I know it well. That scent takes me back. It makes me instantly hard.

"I'm not a product of the wine or your imagination, Eryn."

"You have to be. You look like West. You sound like him. You're hot like him." She shakes her head. "But my sister knows better than to let you into my place. Echo!"

"She's gone. She'll call you in the morning. It's just us here...and what I assume is a sausage, mushroom, and onion pizza." At least based on the savory aroma. "I came to talk to you."

Her eyes narrow. "I don't care that fake-you remembers what I like to eat. Go. You're not welcome here."

"We have to talk." I approach with slow steps.

Eryn backs up, shaking her head. "Stop."

I do.

She snorts. "Now I know you're not real. Turns out, the West I was engaged to didn't give a shit about me or what I wanted."

No doubt she saw it that way. "Can we sit down and eat? Be civil? I'd like to apologize and explain why I'm here. Will you listen?"

E R Y N

I blink. Then blink again.

Nope, Weston Quaid is still standing in my bedroom, looking really, really real—and really, really gorgeous. He still thinks of me? Ha! I don't believe that for a minute. How can I? Besides, if he wants to apologize, he must be a mirage.

Except...when did my visions of West ever include him sporting a perfectly tailored suit, a well-kept beard, and dark hair cut ruthlessly short?

"I'm not spending tonight with you, especially not an imaginary version. That would make me pitiful. And I'm not. I'm just drunk." I tip the bottle to my lips and imbibe another swallow of the mellow red. "Once I'm sober, you'll be gone."

That kind of depresses me.

How many times have I fantasized that West would show up and say he's sorry? Too many. Still, I'm not listening tonight. If I let myself believe he's actually here to make amends for walking out on our wedding day, I'll cry again. I've already done too much of that.

"Eryn." Softly, he cups my shoulder. "I'm staying until we've talked."

At his touch, I'm uncomfortably aware of a dark, unwelcome heat suffusing my every muscle and nerve. It centers into a throbbing ache in one unmistakable place. The sensations make me feel even more woozy...but I'll never be drunk enough to forget that he was the cause of the most humiliating, heartbreaking time in my life.

The contact also proves he's really, truly standing in the

middle of my bedroom, his gaze fixed on me.

"Why?" On this day, of all days? "If you came to find out whether gullible little Eryn is still a train wreck over the split, you can see I'm fine."

He raises an expressive dark brow at me. "So...it's normal for you to be drunk, wearing your wedding dress, and lamenting about your sad sex life since I've gone?"

"You *heard* that?" As mortification rolls over me, I raise the bottle of wine to my lips for more liquid fortification.

West plucks it from my hand and shoves it onto the dresser behind him, out of my reach. "Eryn, we have a lot to say. Give me an hour. I know you don't owe me anything, but if you'll let me say my piece, I'll leave for good."

"Of course you will. You're an expert at that." I wave a dramatic hand through the air. "I remember all the times I 'gave you an hour' and you made my toes curl. Which was awesome; I'm not gonna lie. But then, after everything? Poof. You were gone with nothing more than an 'I'm sorry, honey.'"

"Eryn—"

"Do you know how many people I had to explain our breakup to? I lost count. At first, I told people about your family emergency, but after a while... What was I supposed to say? You didn't explain why you never came back. So I told people how great it was that we realized we weren't compatible before we exchanged vows. It would have served you right if I'd told everyone you had a raging case of herpes." I huff, still trying to comprehend that the one man I thought I'd love, honor, and cherish forever is standing in front of me. "I mailed back gifts and sent a retraction to the paper about our wedding announcement. I canceled everything—and I didn't want your stupid check. I tore it up and paid for everything myself. And while we're at it, this is yours, too." I march to my nightstand and pull out the burgundy velvet box West gave me one hot July evening. All was perfect with the world then... I toss it at him now, gratified it hits him square in the chest. "Take it and go."

West catches the little box, then opens it to find the engagement ring nestled inside, still sparkling and winking in the light. It always mocks me with what might have been, so I stopped looking at it long ago. Mostly.

He sets it on the bed. "This is yours, Eryn. Keep it. I never expected you to give it back."

"But you never expected to slide the matching wedding band on my finger, either, did you? Now that I know you're filthy rich, I guess you're not too broken up about spending thirty thousand on a ring." When he opens his mouth, I wave his words away. "Whatever you're going to say, I don't care. You and I are ancient history, and nothing will change the fact you turned out to be an asshat whose best talent lies between the sheets." I grit my teeth. "Ugh, I have to stop pumping up your ego. If I could get a decent sex life, that would help, but I'm still better off without you. So just go. I'm going to eat my pizza and watch a marathon of *La Femme Nikita*. Or *Kill Bill*. Blood and guts will make me feel better."

"You hate violent movies."

He remembered that, too. That makes me even sadder. Once upon a time, I swore we were perfect for each other. "Maybe since I learned to hate you, I've learned to love them."

As soon as I spit the words out, I clap my mouth shut. Damn it, I don't want to be combative, emotional, or bitter. Booze and West combined have killed my composure.

No, I threw it out the window. Somewhere in my head, I realize I'm not acting like a grown-up. I'd love to be mad at him for that, too. But it's my fault...with some help from merlot.

"I'm sorry." He pins me with solemn eyes. "That I left you with a mess. That I didn't explain. Most of all, I'm sorry that I hurt you."

His sincerity penetrates my alcohol armor. Tears prick my eyes. God, I don't want to be vulnerable to Weston Quaid ever again. "Fine. Apology accepted. Now will you go away?"

He shakes his head. "I can't."

"This is my non-anniversary celebration. I didn't invite you." I lunge for my wine.

West blocks me. "Did you drink most of this bottle by yourself?"

"Newsflash: I'm over twenty-one now, and you're not my daddy."

His jaw works in irritation. "Can't I simply be concerned?"

He's always had a knack for asking questions that take the wind out of my sails. I'm not ready to not be mad at him. "I don't need your concern."

With a sigh that tells me he's grappling for patience, he finishes the last couple of swallows, then shoves the empty bottle onto the dresser again. "You're too drunk and angry to hear me right now. Come with me."

When he grabs my hand, I jerk out of his grasp. "Where?"

He shakes his head, his gaze confronting me with his

exasperation. "Why does everything between us always have to be a chess match?"

"Because I don't trust well. Three years ago, I poured out all the poor little-girl reasons why—and you still shit on me. So excuse me if I'm not jumping up and down to blindly follow you."

"I deserve that," he admits. "But that doesn't mean I don't want to help you."

"I didn't ask for your help."

"I still feel responsible."

"Don't you dare pity me!"

Suddenly, he tugs me close. I stumble over my own two feet because my equilibrium is shot. I admit, I've had too much to drink, and I shouldn't be trying to make myself feel less sad with twenty-something ounces of wine. As a rule, I hardly drink, which is why this bottle has ruined my mood and disposition.

"That's not what I feel," he insists before he drags me up his body.

It's impossible to miss his erection.

Then he distracts me by lifting me into his arms. The musky, all-male scent of him hits my nose and weakens my knees.

"What are you doing?" I shriek.

"Making sure you don't regret tonight tomorrow." He carries me across the bedroom, kicks open the door to my little walk-in closet, and sets me on my feet mere inches away.

I'm unsteady and I want to blame it all on the vino, but West is the cause of my dizziness. I struggle in the small, shadowed space, even more aware of his masculine scent. His big frame towers above me as he spins me away from him and grips my hip, holding me exactly where he wants me while he tugs the zipper down my back.

I freeze as his breath warms my nape. His heat envelops me. My breathing picks up. My heart races.

Only West has ever made me respond purely like a woman.

I should protest his touch, but in the next moment he engulfs my shoulders with his big hands and glides his fingers down my goose-pimpled arms, easing the dress away from my body.

At his touch, I tighten. I tingle. I swallow hard and scramble to find my brain. Finally, I manage to yank the dress back to my chest and twist from his grasp. "Don't touch me."

He pauses, inhaling sharply. Then he lifts his hands in the air.

Instantly, I feel colder without his touch. The chill infuriates me. Why do I still respond to him?

"I only meant to help." His deep voice sounds low and intimate in the two-by-two space.

No way can I give in to that.

"By undressing me?"

"By getting you out of this delicate white dress before you eat greasy pizza."

"It's not like I'm going to wear it anywhere." On the other hand, he's soberer than I am, so maybe he has a point. If nothing else, the dress holds memories. Not only did my older sister Ella wear it on her wedding day, it's a symbol of all I've lost. I should probably want to burn it.

It's annoying that I don't.

"Fine. Get out so I can change." I shoo him toward the door. "In fact, why don't you leave altogether?"

But I already know he won't. West is on some mission, which means he won't give up until he's good and ready.

"We have things to discuss. I'll be in the kitchen with the pizza, waiting for you."

Of course he's going to commandeer my dinner so I have no choice but to follow him. *Ruthless bastard.*

"Don't start eating without me," I order as I take a step toward the closet door so I can shut it behind him.

Instead of gracefully enclosing myself in privacy, I trip on the lacy gown, over my own two feet, and grab his biceps to keep myself from falling. But it's no use. I only manage to yelp as I drag him down to the floor with me.

Together, we land in an ignominious tangle of limbs and breaths, West somehow on top.

Shock freezes me. Right away, I'm aware of two inescapable facts: One, his erection is still ardently saluting me. Two, it feels much better to be nestled under West than I'd like.

"Get off." I shove at him out of self-preservation.

He doesn't move except to brush a wild strand of hair from my face with a soft stroke of his palm. "Eryn..."

Oh, god. He's going to do or say something seductive that will melt me. That truth is obvious in his too-blue eyes.

I wasn't lying when I told Echo that my non-solo orgasm quotient has been nil since West walked out of my life. But is a batch of screaming climaxes really a good reason to crawl

SHAYLA BLACK

between the sheets again with a total bastard? Hmm. Maybe. Or maybe that's the wine talking. That must be it. I can't admit aloud that I've missed him.

"Why is it, no matter what I do, you wind up on top— literally?" I try to sound mad. "You always had the upper hand during our engagement. But now you've been here five damn minutes, and I'm already at a disadvantage."

I'm prepared for just about any response—except the man rolling us over until he's on his back and I'm splayed on top of him. "Happy?"

Something sharp gathers on my tongue, but he short-circuits my ability to talk when his palms glide down my body, stroking the sides of my breasts, skimming my rib cage, before settling on my hips.

"Thrilled." The word slips out way too breathy.

His earthy, musky scent fills my head again. Our gazes connect, his brimming with a heat that compels me. I try to get up and put distance between us, but I only end up bracing my hands on his shoulders with my thighs straddling his hips. Gently, he tightens his hands on my hips and nudges me against his unflagging erection.

"Honey, come closer." His soft rasp commands me.

God, I want to.

My world narrows until I'm only aware of West. Of the way he looks at me. Of the way his heat seeps through the dress to warm me in places I haven't been aware of in three long years.

Suddenly, he wraps his long, strong fingers around my wrists and tugs my palms from his shoulders until they're flat against the low-shag carpet on either side of his head.

Now our hips are pressed together. My chest hovers just above his. His lips are even closer, and I smell the hint of wine on his breath.

I gulp. My heart slams into overdrive. My strength seems to give out.

Why have I always been weak when it comes to this man? From the first moment he spotted me in that crowded bar until right now, I just can't seem to say no.

"What are you doing to me?" I breathe out.

He doesn't answer, simply caresses his way back up my arms and wraps his fingers around my shoulders. A gentle pull I don't have the strength to resist sends me tumbling until I'm braced on my elbows above him.

Our chests touch. My heart chugs frantically. Our lips are so close that with a simple dip of my head, I could experience again just how dizzying it feels to be swept up in Weston Quaid's kiss.

I need to get up and away from this man. He confuses me, scrambles my brain, makes me want things I shouldn't. Problem is, the longer we're this close, the more his blue-eyed stare darkens on me—and the less I care about being cautious.

My elbows slip. My breasts crush against his hard chest. My lips are suspended barely a breath above his. I feel everything around me move and sway.

This is it, the kiss I've secretly waited for. God, I couldn't move if I tried. I ache. I need. My head spins.

I close my eyes and surrender to the knowledge that desiring West is unavoidable. I can't wait to feel him all around me—inside me—again.

Once I close the last of the distance between us, there will be no going back. I'll be in his path again. He'll consume me. He'll have the power to turn me inside out.

Even knowing that, I lower my head. Just one more inch, and we won't be apart anymore...

CHAPTER TWO

WEST

Eryn passed out—right on top of me. Last night, there I was, aching, blood roaring, a breath away from kissing her again. Then...merlot ended the moment.

Of course, I didn't go to her apartment for sex. Or even to mend fences, though I wish we could. I keep telling myself it's good nothing happened between us. She would have been too drunk to consent or remember. But ten hours later, I've barely slept and I'm still sporting a serious case of blue balls that masturbating did nothing to cure. All because I'm fixated on my ex—just like I was the first time we met and every moment I spent with her until I ended our engagement.

Damn it, I'd hoped after I saw her again that I'd realize her grip around my heart was all in my head. Nope. The only thing I learned last night was precisely why all my hooking up and swiping right these last three years has been pointless.

I'm still in love with Eryn Hope. And I'm the one man she will never touch again.

"Coffee?" asks a perky waitress wearing denim shorts and a white apron with JAVA AND JACKS emblazoned across the front.

"Please." I'm going to need caffeine—and lots of it—to manage today.

The young woman pours and recites the day's specials. I'm half listening because I'm not here for the food.

"What can I get you?" she asks, pad of paper and pen in hand.

"Steel-cut oatmeal and ten minutes alone with Eryn."

The waitress pauses, eyeing me. "The oatmeal is no problem. My boss... Are you the reason she's in such a crappy mood this morning?"

Probably, but I don't mention that. "Is she hung over?"

"Yes, like a bitch." The little brunette leans in with a conspiratorial whisper. "She almost looked green when she walked in. How did you know?"

I wince. My news today will hardly brighten her mood.

Well, buddy, she already hates you. It can't get much worse than that...

"I'm sorry to hear she's unwell. But I really need a few minutes alone with her. It's urgent."

She shakes her head. "Look, I don't know if you're her latest fling. There have been a few of those since I started working here six weeks ago. But one thing I know for sure? Eryn won't deal with personal stuff on the job. That woman has a work ethic like I've never seen."

That doesn't surprise me. She's always been both focused and fiercely independent. Since she owns this breakfast bistro now, I know she'll do whatever it takes to succeed. And that gives her a great reason to refuse a conversation with her douchebag ex-fiancé.

Too bad I can't take no for an answer.

"I appreciate that, but I'm actually here on business. I have information she needs to know about the renovations in this building."

"Oh." She nods, clearly taking me more seriously. "All right... Do you want your oatmeal or your meeting first?"

"Meeting." I can't put this off any longer. And I doubt I'll be hungry until I get this conversation done.

The waitress nods. "Come with me."

Gripping my coffee, I follow the brunette across the impressively crowded room. It's a good crowd for a Thursday morning. Granted, she purchased a well-established restaurant with a killer location not far off the highway, right next to the ocean. But she's upgraded the interior decor since I was here last and slapped on a fresh coat of exterior paint. She's created breakfast specials that capitalize on the place's reputation for the best pancakes and coffee west of the 405 Freeway.

The waitress leads me around a corner, past the kitchen, then down a hallway until we reach a door with a plaque that says PRIVATE.

She knocks. "Eryn? You got a minute? I got a guy here who needs to see you. Something about the renovations in the building." She turns to me with a whisper. "I didn't get your name."

I shake my head. "She's not aware that I'm her landlord."

And won't she be somewhere between shocked and pissed when I explain that?

As the waitress gives me another head bob, Eryn calls out. "Can't it wait, Jenna? Pretty busy here..."

Jenna turns to me. I shake my head.

"No," she parrots. "Apparently not."

I hear Eryn sigh. "All right. Show him in."

When Jenna reaches for the knob, I stay her arm. "I've got it from here."

"Cool. I've got to get back to my tables. Tips are everything... Let me know when you want that oatmeal."

Since I probably won't be staying long enough to eat it, I peel away ten bucks and hand it to her. "For the coffee and your time."

She gives me a little grin and deposits the bill in her apron. "Thanks."

Then she's gone. And once again, I'm about to be face-to-face with Eryn. This time, while she's sober.

Deep breath. What's the worst that can happen? Thank god murder is still illegal in all fifty states...

I open the door.

Eryn sits at her tiny desk in the cramped space, flanked on two sides by shelves of papers and binders, along with a printer, a computer, and some surveillance equipment. Janitorial supplies are stacked in the corner. A little fan oscillates on her right, mimicking fresh air since she doesn't even have a window to open in this office.

How does she work here six days a week, ten hours a day? I shut the door for privacy, and I'm already feeling vaguely claustrophobic.

My ex clutches a pen, signs some piece of paper in front of her, and speaks without looking up. "Look, I'm really busy, and I was assured when I took possession of this unit that the renovations would be complete in four weeks. This has dragged on way longer. You need to finish this so it stops being a pain in my ass."

"I'm sorry, Eryn." I'm both apologizing for the present and the past, but nothing I say is going to change either. "We really need to talk."

ERYN

I freeze. The voice that haunted my dreams last night now fills my pounding head.

West. Why is he here?

Slowly, I put down my pen and steel myself to look at him—without wanting him. Because I did when he was in my bedroom last night. He put his hands on me, dragged me against his hard body, and whispered with that deep, rough voice in my ear until I shivered... Two minutes with him, and I was ready to get naked.

Pathetic.

I wish I could say the urge is simply lack of orgasm. Horny would be way easier to accept than love-sick. But I've never been in the habit of lying to myself. For whatever reason, West does it for me. My hormones fell into instant lust when we met. My heart started falling for him in that moment, too. If I'm being honest, I'm not sure it ever stopped.

I can't think about that now. I'm working, and if he's come here to hash out some personal issue, he can wait—until the twelfth of never.

Dragging in a bracing breath, I lift my gaze to him. I thought I was prepared to see West. There's no reason the sight of him in a charcoal-gray suit and a crisp white shirt should impact me. But my belly dips and my girl parts clench. And I may have been tipsy last night, but I distinctly remember being on top of him, staring at his lips, and thinking *Yes. Please. Now.*

Merlot is a bad influence.

"What the hell did you tell Jenna to persuade her to— Never mind. You and I don't need to talk anymore. We did enough of that last night. You just need to go away."

West shakes his head. When we were a couple, he was generally easy to get along with. Why is he being such a pain in my ass now? I waited in vain to see him for three years, and suddenly he drops by twice in less than twelve hours?

"I can't," he insists. "I told Jenna what you weren't sober enough to hear last night: I'm your landlord, and there's a problem with the renovations for this building."

"No. My landlord is JMV Property Holdings. I read every word of the lease documentation I assumed when I bought Java and Jacks."

"The previous owners signed their two-year lease with JMV Property Holdings ten months ago. Quaid Enterprises bought JMV Property Holdings in May."

"And I purchased this place in June."

The pen falls from my fingers and clatters onto my desk. I won't ask if he's kidding. I see he's not.

Son of a bitch.

"Why wasn't I informed?"

"Letters were sent." His eyes fall on the unopened mail I've been meaning to get to on the corner of my desk. "Maybe it's in that stack?"

Maybe. None of it looked important, and I've been crazy busy, so I piled the heap out of my way, waiting for a slow day that never came. "I assume everyone in the building will be notified in writing about the renovation issues?"

"Later today, yes."

"But you decided to tell me in person?" *Why?*

He dips his head, watching me clutch the pen tightly. "I felt I owed you an explanation, in case you were aware I now owned your building. I didn't want you feeling as if I was dragging out the construction to intentionally rub salt in your wound."

I force myself to lean back in my chair in a pose far more relaxed than I feel. "I don't have a wound where you're concerned, Mr. Quaid."

Yes, I'm lying through my teeth, but a girl has her pride.

"I know what happened between us couldn't have been easy on you, Eryn. You may never believe this, but it wasn't easy on me, either."

"Since you sauntered out without a backward glance, it didn't look too hard."

"You're wrong. Leaving you was—"

"In the past. It doesn't matter anymore. Tell me what you came to say, then you can consider your duty done and march back down the hall the way you came."

West clenches his jaw. I'm getting to him. I want to be glad. Instead, I just feel guilty. He's come all the way from— does he still live in New York?—wherever he calls home these days just to tell me whatever he thinks I need to hear. He could have been an asshole and sent me the same written notice the rest of the tenants will receive. As much as I hate to give him props, it was admittedly decent of him to notify me in person.

"All right." He nods abruptly. "The contractor originally hired to complete the seismic retrofit the city insists on had a heart attack before he could finish the job. He's shut down his business until he makes a full recovery. No time frame for that. In the meantime, the city came to inspect the work he already completed. Their structural engineer is insisting on changes that will force us to tear down some walls and reinforce both interior beams and footings. Because the city's deadline is looming, we've hired someone else, but he needs us to close down every unit in the building for the next six weeks in order to complete the work."

I feel the blood leave my face. *"Six weeks?* How the hell do you expect me to make money to live? I have bills to pay. Responsibilities. Some of us weren't born into a family fortune, you know."

"I won't be charging rent for the remainder of the construction."

"Okay, but I will literally have no money coming in. How do you expect me to eat? Pay the rent on my apartment?" I think through the bills in my drawer. "Shit. I have to help my sister with her upcoming spring tuition."

"Believe me, shutting tenants down isn't my first choice. I tried hard to argue with the city to extend the deadline, but they refused. Earthquake safety is nothing to wait on, in their estimation."

I want to be angry. Furious, even. But I've lived here my

whole life. Usually, the ground shaking is merely a tremor—the price you pay for living in SoCal. But when it's not... Well, buildings not up to code can sustain major damage and seriously endanger lives. West is merely complying with the city council's ordinance that requires all buildings to bring their construction up to current standards. I know I can't throttle the messenger...but I can certainly blame him for lots of other things.

I cross my arms over my chest. "How long have you known I'm your tenant?"

"Since you bought the restaurant."

Of course. Very little gets past West. I can't decide whether I'm glad he didn't approach me before now or hurt that he didn't. "When does the new crew start?"

"Monday."

"So I have almost no time to stop shipments or find other ways to save money so I can survive while my place of business is shut down? And how will I pay my employees? Or even keep them? You may not understand that some people live paycheck-to-paycheck, but if they can't make any money for six weeks, then Jenna and all the others will find another job. And when I open my doors again, no one will be around to cook or serve the food. But I guess that's okay because I won't have any customers left, either. They will all have found somewhere else to have their morning coffee and meet with friends or business associates over a short stack. What will you do to me when I can't pay January's rent?"

Regret tightens the strong angles of his face. For a minute, I'd been so angry that I forgot how hot West is or how much I once loved him. It's really unfair that all he has to do is glance my way for me to remember.

"Like I said, I'm sorry. If I had all the answers or a better solution..."

But he doesn't. Honestly, I don't expect him to solve my problems. Hell, I don't expect anyone to do that except me. But it sure would have been nice if he wasn't throwing more challenges in my face. I'm already barely scraping by. The previous owners were an older couple, and once their children started their own lives and stopped helping with Java and Jacks, the place began to run down. I've put every dime I could spare since I took ownership into improvements. I plan to be here for a good, long while. But that means my savings are shot. West's announcement couldn't have come at a worse possible time.

I stand. I want him gone now. I have a lot of problems to solve, and I don't think very well when I'm sharing a four-by-four space with my ex and his manly scent is clouding my head. "There was a time I trusted you to help me with my problems, but that's long over. Just go."

This new, more stubborn version of West doesn't leave. In fact, he leans against the door and slants a glance my way. "I regret us meeting again under these circumstances. I regret even more the way I left you three years ago. As long as I'm here, I think we should talk about it."

"Pass." There's nothing I need less than to dissect the most painful period of my life with the man who caused my misery when I've already got a mountain of other shit to deal with, thanks to his bombshell.

"Aren't you even curious to know why I didn't come back?"

Is he kidding? "I can fill in the blanks. Your family found out about our intimate little wedding, and since your grandfather was ailing, you decided that was a good excuse to ditch the poor, uneducated girl, move back home, and take control of Quaid Enterprises. You picked tradition and a few billion dollars over me. I get it."

"You don't," he insists. "That's not what happened at all."

"At the end of the day, you left me hours before our wedding, flew back to New York, and I never heard from you again until last night. Since it was all over the news, the world knew when you officially became head of Quaid Enterprises a few months back. But let's be real; you've been helming the company since not long after you left me. All the hoopla and press coverage was just about you officially getting those three little CEO letters on your business card. Oh, and I especially loved seeing you on TMZ the week after our breakup with that vapid blonde while you two were on your 'exciting' date to the theater. Did she bang you on the first night, like me? I'll bet she did. After all, you have a way of persuading women out of their clothes."

"I'm sorry for everything. I want to explain—"

"Why? It won't change anything."

"What will it take to get past your anger?"

His question crawls up my back. As if this resentment is somehow my fault? "For you to leave."

"Besides that. Do you want to know that I still have feelings for you?"

"No."

But if he doesn't...why is he all but admitting that he does? Worse, why does his confession melt me even a little?

"Yes, you do. So I'll confess... I still care. After seeing you, I can't deny it."

To my horror, he rounds my desk and invades my personal space. I jump from my chair and try to retreat, but I've got nowhere to go. My office is tiny, and my back hits the shelves. I'm stuck.

"What do you want? Get away." I try to glare, but he studies me as if he can see through my bluster. As if he's well aware he makes me jittery and hot.

The bastard leans closer, so I have to tilt my head back to meet his stare. Then he grabs the shelf above my head with one hand. The other grips the edge of my desk, inches from my hip.

Oh, god. He's surrounding me. This is dangerous.

"I think that's the last thing I should do," he murmurs.

"If you're under the mistaken impression that I'll be an easy lay because I stroked your sexual ego while I was drunk, I won't."

"I never thought that, Eryn."

"Then why are you still here? Are you hard up or just bored?"

"Stop trying to pick a fight. I won't go away until we've cleared the air."

"You already screwed me over romantically, and now you're on your way to ruining me financially. Regardless of whatever feelings you claim to have, there's nothing left between us except regret and loathing."

"There's a lot of regret, I agree. But loathing? Not buying it, honey."

"Don't call me that." It reminds me too much of lying in his arms while he stroked my skin lazily after we reached mutual screaming satisfaction.

West goes on as if I didn't speak. "Loathing doesn't make your eyes dilate, your breath quicken, or your nipples harden. Are you wet for me, too? I'd bet money you are."

No way am I answering that question. "You aren't trying to nail me, I hope."

"That's not my intention..."

But if I offered, he wouldn't turn me down.

"What do you want, West?"

"Honestly? You."

Resistance and desire tangle up inside me. How can I want someone I know is so bad for me? "It's not mutual."

"You're lying. You want to hate me every bit as much as I'm telling myself I should stay away. But this"—he gestures between us—"our chemistry, it's crazy strong. It's not going away simply because we find it inconvenient."

He's right, and my denials only make me sound ridiculous. And terrified. "That doesn't mean we should act on it. We crashed and burned once. Let's not risk it again."

West leans even closer. My breath catches.

"It might turn out differently this time." His voice sounds low and intimate in the small space. "What's the worst that could happen?"

Does he not know how horribly he broke my heart? How badly it's still broken? Maybe not. It didn't truly register with me until I attended Ella's wedding six weeks ago. I cried tears of happiness for her sudden marriage to Carson Frost...and afterward, I sobbed for myself, so full of what-might-have-beens with West.

"What's the best that could happen?" I counter. "A few orgasms, sure. But then?" A lot of pain and tears. "Nothing good. I'm not interested."

He caresses the hair from my face like he can soothe away my protests. "Or maybe something far better than either of us expects. And if not, after the dry spell you've had, are you really so eager to turn down those orgasms?"

My answer doesn't come as swiftly or as confidently as I'd like. "Yes."

"I don't believe you."

Suddenly, his thighs bracket mine. One of his palms envelops my hip. The other cups my nape. God, he's everywhere. My heart slams against my ribs. My breaths turn shallow and harsh. I don't know what to do with my hands, and somehow my fingers find their way to his steely biceps. When he tilts his head down, my eyes slide shut. I should be screaming in protest. Instead, I tremble for the kiss of the only man I've ever loved.

He doesn't swoop in and take my mouth in a heated rush. No, he's patient as he inches his lips toward mine, giving me a hundred opportunities to stop him. But my entire body is suddenly focused on him like a divining rod. I can't stand Weston Quaid. I definitely shouldn't want him. And yet I *need* to feel him now.

Over the last three years, every time I dug my nails

into another man's back, I willed myself to feel even half the pleasure West gave me. I never did because I was still hung up on the man I almost married.

If I peel back all the bluster and BS I've buried myself under, I'm still hung up on him.

There, I admitted it. Maybe I needed to do that in order to move on. Maybe that's part of getting him out of my system. Letting him kiss me might be, too.

Yes, I'm rationalizing, but I still tilt my chin up to him, purse my lips, sink my fingers into his arms.

"Eryn..." he murmurs an inch above my lips.

Then he stops, utterly still, his entire body taut. I'm pinging with anticipation for him to kiss me already.

But he doesn't.

A dozen seconds slide by before I realize he's waiting for me to close the last inch between us. If I want his mouth on mine—and I seriously do—I have to make the last move.

It's too late to question the wisdom of this decision. I lift onto my tiptoes and press our lips together.

Oh, my god. I'm kissing Weston Quaid again.

It's hesitant at first. Then, suddenly, it's a wildfire. Feeling his mouth on mine is heaven, homecoming, perfection. It's like every memory of our passion that's haunted my dreams. His scent fills the air with the olfactory equivalent of crack. His touch almost makes me weep.

He tightens his grip on me an instant before he takes command of our kiss, lifting me onto the desk and spreading my legs by wedging his body in between, and holding me there as if he's determined never to let me go. I'm still trying to catch my breath and process what's happening when he plunges his tongue into my mouth, scoops my ass in his hands, and presses his erection against my wet ache.

West used to be a patient and playful lover, often finding clever ways to undo me. The man kissing me now is a possessive demon. He rocks against me in silent demand. The force of his lips and his will tilts my head until he's able to penetrate my mouth even deeper. He sends my head whirling, my heart thudding, and my sex weeping for more.

My ex is more than melting me. I'm about to disintegrate. In this moment, nothing matters except wrapping my legs around him. Well, except maybe getting my mouth somewhere on him. Anywhere. I need to taste the combined tang of his salty skin and his male musk I've never forgotten.

I end our kiss and trail my lips across his jaw, then lick my way down to his neck. Yes, that flavor I've craved is right here, so strong and potent. It sends my head spinning. But his groan at the feel of my mouth on him soars my arousal to another level. He might be unraveling me, but I'm getting to him, too.

"Fuck, Eryn." He tosses his head back and growls in the too-small space. "I need more of you."

He drags my shirt down to expose my shoulder. I arch closer, clinging. His mouth caresses my bare skin instantly, tongue laving, teeth dragging. I gasp at the sensations. It's not anything another man hasn't done to me, but when West works his magic, it's somehow totally new.

"Feel good?" he rasps. "Yeah... I want to do this to your nipples, too. Kiss them, suck them deep, bathe them with my tongue. Then I want to work my way down your body, get my mouth on your pussy, eat at you until you cry out my name as you come."

Yes. Now!

I fumble with the buttons of his dress shirt, kissing my way across his shoulder as I uncover an expanse of his golden, hair-roughened chest. The more I expose, the more I gape. West was always well put together, but he's clearly developed a hard-core gym habit since I last saw him naked.

"Oh, my god..." I breathe.

The man was always my fantasy, but now he's even hotter. How am I going to resist him?

Why would I even want to?

There's a reason, but I can't remember it right now. And it doesn't matter. Only getting my tongue on that flat, male nipple an inch out of my reach is important.

With frantic hands, I shove his coat off his shoulders, gratified when I hear it fall to the floor. But I'm too busy tugging at the starched white cotton preventing me from seeing his bare torso to celebrate. "I want you naked."

"You first," he moans as he drags my T-shirt up my ribs and over my breasts.

Reluctantly, I stop touching him long enough to lift my arms. Then he's tearing the cotton from my body and tossing it across the room. Cool air hits my skin. We breathe hard. Our panting fills my office as he loosens the last few buttons of his shirt and shrugs out of it, losing it somewhere on my cluttered desk behind him.

And I get my first unobstructed look at him.

Holy shit.

West doesn't pause to let me eye-fuck all the ripples and hard swells of his strong shoulders, defined pecs, or that new six-pack. No, he's already peeling back the lacy cups of my bra and tucking them under my aching breasts. They bulge up— inches from his waiting mouth.

"I've dreamed of these." His hot breaths bathe my taut nipples as he cups the swells.

Mouth open, he draws one of the buds against his tongue and circles it before pulling deep. Friction. Suction. Pressure. The trifecta of nipple Shangri-la.

My head falls back, giving him more access to the breasts he's determined to devour. I grip his head, fingers digging into his scalp, silently begging him to never stop.

Our moans and harsh breaths grow louder. I need him closer. I'm desperate to feel every inch of his naked skin pressed to every inch of mine. This hard surface isn't comfortable now—and it definitely won't be if we get horizontal, but that's hardly my biggest concern. If we lose the rest of our clothes, nothing will matter except the pleasure. I've needed this kind of undeniable, incendiary passion for years. I've craved it. I've missed West enough to know.

But what's changed between us?

Absolutely nothing.

He reaches for the snap of my jeans. If I don't stop this, in a few short jerks, I'll be totally naked in front of the only man who's ever hurt me. The only man I've ever given that power to.

I fear he still has that power.

Gasping, I give him a mighty shove and right my bra, ignoring my protesting nipples. "Don't touch me again. Get out."

He gapes, looking dazed, like he's struggling to downshift and understand my sudden refusal. "Eryn, I—"

"No. This was stupid. *I* was stupid. You have no business touching me. You gave up that right when you walked out."

But I'm painfully aware that I instigated our kiss. I have to blame myself, too.

Hands on his hips, West breathes hard and stares at me. I force myself not to look at his muscled torso, rippling with even his smallest move. It's hard not to look, though. Harder still not to ache for him, because even if my head knows better than to let this man touch me, my body doesn't care. It's screaming at me to forget both the past and the future and to let West give me a good time right now.

No, no, no. Why can't I purge him from my hormones? Or is my heart the traitor here?

"I regret losing you every single day."

I scramble for my shirt and tug the garment over my head. "You had a funny way of showing it. Not that it matters anymore. You came here to tell me about the building construction. Now I know. Thanks so much. There's the door. Don't let it hit you on the way out."

With a long sigh, West reaches for his shirt and shrugs it over his shoulders. "Do you think for one instant it's that simple, Eryn? Do you really think these last five minutes won't haunt you tonight?"

I want to insist they won't, but why lie when we both know the truth?

Barely able to look in his direction, I jump off the desk and sidestep him. "We're over, and this is done. Goodbye, West."

Instead of letting me go, he grabs my arm and pulls me back into his body, murmuring in my ear, "We're *not* done. You haven't seen the last of me, honey. That's a promise."

CHAPTER THREE

WEST

"Got a minute?" I ask, calling my sister from Java and Jack's parking lot.

Genevieve Quaid is a force all her own. Shrewd, beautiful, elegant. She's had a scrape or two with love, so she understands the scars. Besides, few people know me better—or can give me more astute advice. I need it. My instinct to simply rip off Eryn's clothes and remind her repeatedly how amazing we are together in bed won't win her back.

I hear Gen turn off the music in the background and shift the phone in her grasp. "What's going on? And where are you? I called your office this morning. Mary said you were out for the rest of the week."

"I'm in LA." I pause because I know my announcement will shock my sister. "I've been trying to talk to Eryn."

"That's interesting. And?"

"I drove out here purely for business...but I don't think I can walk away from her again."

"I'm not surprised. The first time almost killed you." She hesitates. "No offense, but she's good for you, and you're a miserable bastard without her."

"None taken. You're right. I called you because I need help untangling the female psyche—or rather, Eryn's stubborn resistance—before I proceed."

"She didn't welcome you, I take it?"

"I think she would have preferred a case of the clap."

Gen laughs. "I'm not surprised. But look on the bright side. You haven't lost your sense of humor."

"I'm serious about this." I have to be. That kiss we shared in her office... It's the most alive I've felt in three years.

Still, if I thought I was the only one hung up after our separation, I'd do my damnedest to leave my ex in peace. I put Eryn through a lot, and in her shoes, without knowing what truly caused our split, I wouldn't give me a second chance, either. But that five minutes in her office tells me our flame still scorches hotter than ever. And given everything she told Echo last night under the influence of vino, she hasn't moved on. God knows I haven't.

Since I'm the one who broke us, shouldn't I be the one to put us back together?

"But if she doesn't want you in her life, what are you going to do? You can't force her to accept you."

Now Gen is understanding my dilemma. "I need a strategy."

"Have you tried simply explaining?"

"She's not ready to hear it. She doesn't trust me. So why would she believe me?" I suspect she's afraid the truth will change her mind, and she can't yet handle the possibility of caring about me again.

"I get that. So what *is* she willing to talk about?"

"The best conversation we've had since I knocked on her door last night..." I wince. "Well, there wasn't a lot of talking."

She gasps. "You did *not* take her to bed before mending fences. West!"

"I didn't." But if she hadn't protested in her office? I absolutely would have.

As much as I hate to admit it, having sex with Eryn before we've resolved anything would have been a mistake.

"Why do I get the feeling it was a close call? I don't want details, mind you," Gen rushes to tell me.

Yeah. Just no on the TMI with my sister. "After a pair of run-ins with Eryn, I feel as if I've got two options to proceed: I either stroll her down memory lane and make her remember all the reasons we fell in love in the first place."

"That's stupid. Next?"

"Thanks for giving the idea a chance," I drawl.

"Every time you try that tactic, she'll mentally bump into 'The End.' Until you explain why you left, you'll never win her trust again. And you won't progress her beyond a hot moment or two. As I recall, chemistry was *never* the problem with you two."

Gen is right. I just don't know how to tell Eryn when she refuses to listen.

"What's your other choice?" my sister prompts.

"Coercion. I'm not proud of it, but if I *make* her listen—"

"She probably still won't hear you. And even if she does, will she get it?"

That's a valid question. The situation that forced me to leave Eryn is ugly and complicated.

"Maybe she needs to see all the crap for herself," Gen says.

My first reaction is to tell my sister she's finally gone crazy. First, despite my suggestion, I wonder if I can make Eryn breathe unless she wants to. Second, I hate to put her in the middle of the shit show. Then my brain starts turning and my thoughts begin churning. Maybe there is a way to work this out...

"What's going on with Uncle Eddie?" I ask.

"I haven't seen him lately, but I'm convinced he's up to something. I hear rumors..."

"I already know he's making another play for my job." And I'll be damned if I let him take from me what I've fought so hard to win. "Is he still in Vegas?"

"I don't know. When he is, he usually maintains a high profile, but he's been awfully quiet the last couple of weeks." I hear the concern in her voice. "If he's gunning for you, little brother, it's serious. And personal. Mom won't take Eddie's challenge or Eryn's return well, either."

"I'll deal with her. Heard anything from anyone else on the board?"

"No, but I worry there are some under-the-table dealings going on," Gen warns. "The board meeting is only two weeks away, and I have no doubt our dear uncle is actively plotting against you. You need to get home ASAP."

"My gut says the same." I have to stop him. I probably shouldn't wait until Sunday to head home, but if I leave Eryn now, what little bit of her animosity I've been able to thaw will freeze again. "If you hear anything, let me know."

"Will do. Are you thinking of ways to get Eryn to Vegas?"

Sometimes, Gen is so smart I swear she's a mind reader. "Yeah, and I think I've got an idea how."

I hope she doesn't hate me for it...but—at least for the short term—I'm not holding my breath.

ERYN

This morning did not go well. Waking up hung over and still aching for West was bad enough. Almost having sex with him in my office... *So* not smart.

After he left, I couldn't spend another moment in there for the rest of the workday. Instead, I donned an apron and waited tables until the last of the lunch crowd left. The rush left me little time to think, but once the doors closed at two and I scrubbed the place clean...I found myself alone with my thoughts.

To escape them, I gave my long-neglected gym membership a workout. I also hit the grocery store, dialed Echo to chew her out but settled for her voice mail instead, made some phone calls to suspend food and supply shipments for Java and Jacks, then reached out to some local contacts about a job for the next six weeks. Finally, I gave in to my urge for a hot shower and a power nap.

Now, it's eight p.m., and I'm wide awake. This is close to my usual bedtime since my alarm is usually set for four a.m. But tonight I'm too keyed up for sleep.

It's West's fault.

Behind me, my phone buzzes. A glance at the device tells me I have a fifth missed call from him. I listen to one of his messages. He wants to see me, says it's urgent.

48

By his own admission, we've concluded the business between us. The only burning issue left is our enduring mutual lust. The question is, do I ignore his message...or pursue it? God, I'm crazy to even consider the question.

I pace and chew on a ragged nail. But my thoughts keep circling back to one realization: if I want my ex out of my life for good, I can't manage that by willing myself to forget him. I know that doesn't work because I've already tried. For years.

What I haven't tried? Fucking him out of my system.

With a frustrated sigh, I reach for my phone, then hesitate. Am I being impulsive? Probably, but does that automatically make this idea wrong? After all, if I don't call him, what are my more appealing options to forget him?

Sex it is.

Blistering excitement twists my belly. I try to write it off as nerves as I press the button to return my last missed call.

West picks up on the first ring. "Eryn?"

"Why are you calling me?"

"I've got a proposition for you." His voice sounds smoky and thick. Sexy. Or am I hearing what I want in his tone? Whatever the case, his rasp wrenches my anticipation higher.

"I've got one for you, too." After this morning's kiss, I'm going to guess my proposition is a lot like his. "Can you be here in ten minutes?"

"Five. I'm not far."

I start questioning the wisdom of my decision again, but it's too late. I've opened the door, and knowing West, he'll charge in like a bull. "Have you eaten?"

"I haven't thought about food."

Gripping the phone tighter, I struggle for breath. "Me either."

"Be ready."

Three beeps let me know he's hung up.

My heart shifts into overdrive. I toss the device on the sofa. My thoughts race as I rush to my bedroom and tear into a drawer I haven't opened in months. Finally finding what I'm looking for, I toss on the skimpy garments and throw a robe over myself, just in case I'm wrong about his intentions.

As I'm belting it closed, I hear his fist bang on my door, heavy and insistent.

With my belly seizing and my sex clenching, I dash across the unit to let him in. "That was fast."

"This can't wait."

He shuts and locks the door behind him with a sure flick of his wrist. Then he pivots, fixes his stare on me, and stalks in my direction.

I back away into the living room, more nervous than I want to be. "What's your proposition?"

"You first."

"All right." Clenching my fists, I work up my nerve. "I want you to fuck me. Tonight and tonight only."

If he's surprised, he hides it well. "So this is a booty call?"

"Yes. Nothing else."

"Why?"

Why do I want him, or why is it just sex? "Everything I said when I was drunk is true. No one makes me feel as good in bed as you. This morning proved we're hotter than ever together. You want it. I want it. We're consenting adults." I shrug. "Why not?"

West's expression gives away nothing. "Valid points. I've never ached for another woman the way I do for you. On a lot of levels, sex makes sense."

I try not to let my relief show as I unbelt my robe. "Exactly. Let's get to it. My bedroom."

"Wait." He grabs my wrist. "I have a slightly different proposition."

"What?"

"Tell me, if we have sex tonight, what happens tomorrow? Do we just go our separate ways?"

My first inclination is to say yes, then I reconsider. What if I haven't completely scratched my itch for him by then? "We can make that decision in the morning."

"No. I've waited three years to feel you again. I already know a few hours won't do," he insists. "And I can't stay in LA. I need to get home."

"Where's that?"

"Vegas. Come with me."

Is he crazy? "I have a life here. A business."

"That will be shut down for the next six weeks."

"Not until after my Sunday rush."

"Fair enough. Come to Vegas then."

I yank from his grip and pace. "So, you're suggesting... what? That for the six weeks Java and Jacks is shut down, we fuck our brains out? Or until we get tired of each other? I can't do that, West. I need a temporary job to make ends meet."

"I'm not making myself clear. Let me try again." He reaches into his coat pocket and withdraws a fat sealed envelope and a pen, then drops both on my entry table. "This is a contract. I've already signed it. If you agree to the terms, I will pay the salary of every one of your employees for the duration of the remaining construction. In addition to waiving your rent, I will pay you your estimated lost revenue plus ten percent for that same period. In exchange, you will come to my home—to my bed—and be my mistress."

My jaw drops as shock pings through me. I belt my robe tightly again. "You can't buy me; I'm *not* a whore."

"You're not," he assures. "I'm proposing an equitable solution to our mutual problem. I have no choice but to shut you down temporarily. But I'm willing to be fair. During this unavoidable construction, you pointed out that you have employees to retain and bills to pay, which you can't do without money coming in. This arrangement takes care of that. And while the contractor brings the building up to code, you and I can deal with the fact that we still want each other. I can't be away from the office for six weeks, so the ten percent extra is to compensate you for the inconvenience of being away from home."

As much as I hate to admit it, his proposition makes a warped sort of sense. I hate even more how tempted I am. The only way I've experienced Vegas is with six girls in one cramped Motel 6 room for a night shortly after I turned twenty-one. That was a haze of vodka, smoke, and bad decisions, so I don't remember much. But the city aside... What about having six weeks of toe-curling, spine-melting, blood-boiling sex with West? That should give me plenty of time to work him out of my system. Maybe then I can return to LA and forget about the past. Yes, and with my slate clean, I'll be able to focus solely on the future.

Isn't that what I've wanted every time I've been masochistic enough to grab a bottle, don my wedding dress, and succumb to tears?

The twinges of missing my ex aside, yes.

What happens if you fall in love with him again?

I shove the pesky voice aside. I know him now, which means I'll know better than to lose my heart. When he first sweet-talked me, I was a cynical twenty-year-old, hoping deep down that Prince Charming would sweep me off my feet and prove me wrong. Now I know true love really is just another fairy tale. I won't fall for West's bullshit twice.

I look for other flaws in the plan, but I don't have pets or any other responsibilities to hold me in LA. My sisters may not approve, but they won't try to stop me. Plus, not having to wake up every day at four in the morning or wait someone else's tables, even temporarily, is really, really appealing.

"What am I supposed to do all day while you're working?"

"Whatever you want. Rest. Shop. Relax. There's a full spa in my building, a mall less than half a mile away, and a cache of movies, music, and books in my condo. You shouldn't be bored. But listen to me, Eryn." He grabs my chin. "You'll be mine between six p.m. and six a.m."

My heart slams against my ribs. "And you'll be mine."

A little smile plays across his face. "Is that a yes?"

I don't want to make this too easy on him. True, I already asked him for sex tonight, but I only had to give myself for a couple of hours. This is a month and a half of being in West's arms, indulging in every pleasure that makes me shiver and sigh.

I yank from his grip. "I need to read the paperwork first."

"You should. There are conditions."

"Like what?"

"First, when we're alone in my apartment, you're naked. Always. Second, wash your hair or take care of any 'headaches' before I get home every night, because I don't want to hear excuses. When I walk in the door, I only want to hear you say 'yes.'"

I don't see an ounce of humor on his face. So clearly, he's serious. The idea of surrendering to West on that level is both thrilling and scary as hell.

"Do I get to sleep?"

"You'll have all day to nap, honey."

Holy cow, that should *not* turn me on. "Anything else I should be aware of before I decide?"

He nods. "We'll be having dinner with my family once."

I feel my eyes go wide. West's siblings Flynn and Genevieve aside, I've never met the infamous Quaid clan. Sure I've seen pictures and read tabloid accounts, but he never introduced us when we were engaged. And I always found that odd. Then again, I was never more than his dirty little secret. "Why?"

"Because it's necessary. Since you'll be with me and I don't want to be without you, you'll come along."

Something about his excuse doesn't ring true, but I don't know what he's actually up to, so I can't refute him. And maybe it doesn't matter. So we'll have a stilted meal on gilded plates with some of his famous relatives. Whatever...

"Fine." I send him a slow, heavy-lidded stare. "What about tonight?"

He shakes his head with regret. "I need to be back in the office tomorrow morning. I've been away from my responsibilities too long as it is."

"So you're saying if I want you at all, I have to sign your contract and come to Vegas?"

"Yes." He steps closer and wraps an arm around me. "But I'm happy to leave you something to think about."

He dips his head and covers my lips with his. I should probably resist on principle, but my head gives way to my long-starved libido and the internal war I wage ends in an embarrassingly short skirmish.

I melt around West, opening my mouth to him, curling my arms around his neck. Hell, I even rub myself against him. He exploits my weakness swiftly and without mercy, plunging deeper into the kiss while thumbing his way across my aching nipples. I writhe. I mewl. I give in utterly. He takes in my surrender as if it's his right, lifting me against his massive frame and carrying me to the living room sofa.

The moment I'm flat on my back, he tugs open the belt of my robe and shoves the garment wide. His eyes nearly bulge from their sockets. "Holy shit... I've forgotten how gorgeous you are in black lace."

I knew this outfit would get to him. He's always had a thing for me in anything delicate and sheer. But this low-cut, breast-hugging babydoll trimmed in little pink bows has him panting. Good. He can't always have the upper hand.

With a coy flutter of my lashes, I smile. "Are you just going to stare at me or actually do something?"

"Always pushing me, always trying to take control. You're a bad girl, Eryn. I definitely intend to do something."

Before I can question what, he wraps his fingers around the filmy sides of my panties and yanks them down my thighs. I'm still gasping when he unbuttons the single closure holding my babydoll together.

That quickly, I'm totally bare to his gaze. He drinks me in hungrily as he shoves my thighs apart. "A landing strip?"

In the past, West loved it when I waxed bare. He'd heap hours of enjoyment on me. The maintenance wasn't a hardship when the benefits were so awesome. But after he left, I let myself go natural again. I only shaved this design a few hours ago. Why not? I told myself. But on some level, I knew he would see it. And I knew it would provoke a response.

I shrug casually. "It's my body. I can do whatever I want with it."

"If you sign the agreement, your body is *mine* for the next six weeks. Get rid of this before you come to Vegas." He swipes a thumb through the patch of curls before settling the digit over my clit. "Are we clear?"

I fight not to squirm and beg him for more.

"What if I don't want to?" I hear the breathy defiance in my voice.

His smile is slow and smug. "Still like playing this game, honey?"

The one where I goad and tempt him into teasing me until I beg and twist and dissolve into a million pieces at his feet? "No game. Merely asking a question."

SHAYLA BLACK

"Well, if you don't play nicely, I might not feel like doing this." He yanks my hips onto the arm of the sofa and kneels between my thighs, his breaths pelting my flesh, before he licks his way through my saturated sex with a groan.

God, that's so good. By definition, oral sex should be. But I've been single enough in the last few years to know that's not always the case. Some guys fumble this. Or pass on it altogether. West is really focused and really talented at making me combust.

As he prods my clit with the tip of his tongue, I arch and lift to him. He parts me with his thumbs and devours me with his whole mouth. It's as if I've been revved back to life, like I was dead and his tongue is the jolt of pleasure I needed to awaken my senses once more.

"You still taste so sweet..." he murmurs before he lowers his head again.

He's unrelenting when it comes to ramping me up. As if his mouth isn't enough, he also brushes my most sensitive spots with his fingers and watches me slowly come unhinged with a satisfaction that arouses me even more.

"Can you see what I'm doing to you?"

"Yes," I breathe.

"Can you feel what I'm doing to you?"

"Yes."

"Can you stop yourself from pleading with me to do more?"

No, I can't. *Damn him.* "West!"

"Answer me." He toys with me, his voice a tease all its own.

The pleasure is so strong, it's agony. I have no defense

against it, no way to fight it. Breathing through it does nothing. Flowing with it only spins my head until I feel as if I'm dizzy and drowning in a pool of ecstasy.

Then he ceases every seductive movement and pulls away. "I'll stop. Weren't you protesting for that when you called my name?"

The sly bastard knows better, and I hate him for toying with me. But if I don't admit how much I want him, he'll let me weep and die from the unfulfilled pleasure.

"Don't stop," I gasp out. "Don't... I can't take it. You make me ache. Please."

The smile that slides across his face is both sexual and terrifying. He knows he's got me. I'll care later. Right now, I don't.

"You're sure you want more?" He licks his lips with a hum.

I nod and grab a handful of his shirt to yank him closer. "Yes. Damn you, yes!"

He lets loose a satisfied laugh. "Glad to hear it. I'd hate to bore you." Then he shrugs out of my grip and stands with a seemingly reluctant sigh. "But I would never want you to feel as if I'm wringing a response from you while you're under duress. Maybe I should give you time to think about whether you really want me. You can let me know on Sunday."

"C'mon. You can stay another ten minutes."

West shakes his head. "I can't. Come to Vegas. We'll have a nice dinner. You can tell me then if you'll be signing my contract and accepting my offer or walking away for good."

He's going to leave me needing, pleading, and aching like this for *three days*? Of course he is. He knows my weaknesses.

Good sex. Good food. He's laying a trap and daring me to walk right into it. The question is, why?

I struggle to my feet and cover myself. "What do you really want from me, you bastard?"

West cocks his head and smiles as he settles his suit coat back in place. "Come to my place on Sunday, and you'll find out."

CHAPTER FOUR

ERYN

After barely sleeping, I come to a few conclusions. The biggest one is that if I don't play my hand right, I'm screwed. After making a few phone calls to the city verifying West's story about the seismic retrofitting's deadline and the initial contractor's heart attack, I remember that he's not a liar, just a player.

I can't let myself get played again.

On the other hand, when I risk a glance at my bank balance, it's bleeding red. Rent is due in two weeks. I need to make my car payment in three. I can't do any of that unless I act fast.

Beside me, my phone buzzes. I tense, half expecting West to be on the other end, prodding me for an answer. But no, it's my little sister, finally returning my call. As I answer, I can't decide whether I'm disappointed West isn't demanding my attention or annoyed because he's playing some damn cat-and-mouse game.

"Hey, Echo."

"Uh-oh. I know that voice. How bad is it between you and West? I meant to call you yesterday, but the day got away from me."

I'm not sure what to say when I can't seem to untangle it myself. "It's a cluster."

I fill her in, leaving nothing out. Well, almost nothing. I think if I told her how quickly West had me panting, she'd probably berate me. Admitting he kissed me—and that I liked it—is embarrassing enough. I refuse to even think about the throbbing ache he left me with that isn't going away.

"What are you going to do?"

"I'm still weighing my options. But one thing I know? I'm going to kill you for letting him in while I was drunk, then checking out on me like that."

Echo pauses. "You can't kill me. Ella would come unhinged. Besides, I did that because I kinda felt sorry for him."

"Sorry?" Is she kidding? "He's the one who left me."

"I know, and I haven't forgiven him for that. But I also let him in for you. I love you, and I want the best for you."

"What makes you think West qualifies?"

"I don't know that he does. But I've seen you turn some great guys upside down and inside out in the last three years. I don't think you meant to," Echo quickly qualifies. "You always start a relationship well-meaning. But once a guy gets too close, you cut him off at the knees. You weren't that difficult before West. I mean, you were always cautious, and that was fine. Now you're scared. I don't think you can overcome the fear until you deal with your feelings for him."

"You're twenty-one and still a virgin because you're hung up on your superhot best friend. What do you know?" I say dismissively, then feel instantly contrite. She's right, and that was a low blow. I'm sounding like a bitch.

"I'm not hung up on Hayes, and you leave my bestie out of this," she grumbles. "I might not know a lot about adult life, but I know *you*. And you need to deal with your feelings for him, Eryn."

Instead of saying the first sarcastic thing that lands on the tip of my tongue, I bite back the verbal swipe. It won't help anyone, least of all me.

"Sorry. So...going to Vegas to be West's mistress and screwing him out of my system isn't a horrible idea?"

"Weirdly, no. You'll leave at the end of six weeks either knowing that you're finally free of him or irrevocably in love. And I'm pretty sure you'll know how he feels about you, too. Have you thought about that? Asked yourself why he's so insistent on getting you back into his bed? Into his life?"

I have. I just don't know the answer. "West's mind is a mystery, but if I go, I'll be doing it for clarity, so I can leave with an open head and heart."

"Totally. Besides, getting a long, well-paid vacation out of it can't be all bad. And Vegas!"

She makes good points. "Hey, don't you get a fall break from school in a few weeks? You could come visit me."

"I'm not sure West will appreciate me in your shared love nest."

"Well, he can live with it. If I go, promise you'll come out to see me for a few days."

"I'll think about it. Right now, Hayes is talking about some big group camping and canoeing trip to the mountains."

"He doesn't need you to lie on the hard ground to hang out

with his farting, beer-drinking buddies."

"I hear you." But she sounds reluctant to bail on Hayes, and I know that, despite her protests, she's utterly into him. "We'll play it by ear, okay? We've got time to decide. Heck, we don't even know for sure that you're going to Vegas."

"Yeah." But what else is there to think about? If I don't go, won't I always wonder *what if?* "I'll keep you posted."

The rest of the day passes in a blur of activity. I plead my way into thirty minutes with my hairdresser for a fresh cut and style. I hit a nearby brow bar. I get a killer mani-pedi. I find the most amazing bloodred lipstick at the mall. I even do a little lingerie shopping.

One thing I don't do? A damn thing about the landing strip that displeased West so much. If I go to Vegas, I'm doing it to please myself, so I can have the closure I never got when we split up. If he's more hung up on my pubic hair than our relationship, this will be an easy six weeks of hot sex for me. We'll share pleasure, some laughs, and that command performance dinner with his family. Then just before Thanksgiving, I'll be heading home—and leaving West behind for good.

I like that plan.

With a smile, I grab a suitcase and begin tossing things in.

WEST

I pace, phone in hand. It's seven p.m. on Sunday. No sign of Eryn.

My apartment is ready for her arrival. Hell, I've made room for her in every corner of my life. Half my closet and dresser are empty. I've ruminated, planned, grabbed supplies.

And thought long and hard about how to handle her once she walks through the door.

If she comes at all.

It's been almost seventy-two hours since I last laid eyes on her. She still hasn't given me any indication whether she's coming...or whether she's blowing me off. But I'm betting on the former.

But if she doesn't come, the slow, toe-curling seduction I plotted, followed by the long heart-to-heart we need will probably never happen. And that's not acceptable. If I have to drive back to LA and drag that stubborn woman to my penthouse by her hair...

Fuck, I sound like a caveman. That's how Eryn makes me feel—primal and possessive. I *know* she wants me, too. I felt it. I heard it. I made her a damn good offer. The only reason she would refuse is out of spite.

Knowing Eryn, that's enough reason to turn me down.

Why didn't you just tell her you think you might still be in love with her and that you want to try again? My sister asked me that during my drive home Thursday night. The question is valid...but pointless. Eryn wouldn't have believed me. I'm not even sure she would have cared. Somehow, I have to change her mind.

Is six weeks even long enough? Given the armor she's surely built around her heart since I walked away from our wedding, I don't know if six decades would be.

The hum of vague street racket forty floors up from the Strip blends with the crooning of a sultry-voiced female on my radio who sings that she can't help falling in love. The sounds blend together, fade into the background like white noise. I feel how alone I am. How fucking alone I've been since I forced myself to walk away from Eryn.

Suddenly, someone knocks on my door.

My heart stops for a tense second before thudding again. I stride across my unit in a handful of steps and yank the door open, fixing a welcoming smile on my face. Instead of Eryn, I see the delivery person from the nearby restaurant with our food.

"Good evening, Mr. Quaid. Where would you like your dinner?"

"Follow me." Trying not to sound let down, I lead the college-aged guy to my kitchen and turn on the warming drawer under my oven. "Set it on the counter. Put dessert in the refrigerator. I'll take care of the rest."

"My pleasure, sir."

He does as instructed, then hands me a receipt to sign. With a flick of a pen, I pay for the food and wave him toward the door, presuming he can take a hint.

I unpack the meal, double-checking containers and setting the hot items in the warming drawer, when I hear an unexpected voice.

"Well, this is a sight I never thought I'd see. *The* Weston Quaid in the kitchen, looking domestic. Then again, I guess it's not that hard to call for takeout."

Eryn.

I turn toward her. Sure enough, she stands in the entrance of the kitchen, looking way more edible than anything the five-star restaurant just delivered. Her little black spandex top cups her shoulders and breasts—and ends inches above the sensual indentation of her waist. Formfitting black yoga pants expose her naval, hug her hips, and cling to her shapely thighs. It's the sexiest athletic wear I've ever seen.

Finally, I manage to clear my throat and find my voice. "You're here."

"Clearly."

"I didn't hear you knock."

"Because I didn't. The dude delivering food opened the door to leave as I approached. He even held it open for me with a smile."

If he flirted with Eryn, I regret the nice tip I gave him. "Suitcases?"

"In the car. No rush." She shrugs, then looks at the food containers strewn all over my darkened kitchen. "Whatever that is smells good."

"Hungry?"

"Sure. Or, since you're keeping it warm, it can wait." Another shrug. "Whatever."

She's nervous. She wants me to think her mood is very chill and she doesn't have a care in the world, but her eyes look tense, almost too alert. Same with her shoulders. She came here, maybe even against her better judgment. I didn't leave her many options. Sure, she could have waitressed at some dive and spent twelve grueling hours a day on her feet in order to make up the income this seismic reconstruction is costing her. But she's too smart to do that. I'm offering her easy money. It only comes with one itty-bitty catch.

I'm going to do whatever it takes to make her fall in love with me again.

"Dish up the food and pour us some wine. I'll bring up your suitcases."

"Sure." She tosses me her car keys. "Where are the wineglasses?"

I point to the cabinet in the dining room. "I've already set the table."

With a noncommittal nod, Eryn turns to the task at hand. I leave, gritting my teeth. She's determined not to let my effort or seduction matter to her. She definitely doesn't want anything I do to bridge the chasm between us. Does she want a fight? Or is she simply trying to goad me into proving that my desire to have her back is real?

A few minutes later, I return with her luggage. As soon as I dump everything in my bedroom, I race to the dining room to see Eryn sitting at the table, one foot resting flat on the seat of her chair. She's braced her forearm against her upthrust knee, and she's swirling her vino casually in her stemless glass.

"Nice place," she says with a glance around.

It is. It's not exactly the way I want it yet, but it's definitely a giant step up from the shack by the beach we shared a long time ago, when I didn't have any money of my own or any responsibilities except to make decent grades and to show up for the occasional family event.

"Except...it looks more like Liberace lives here than you."

Eryn is poking, trying to get a rise out of me. Oh, she got one, but not my temper. I won't let her prod that over something so petty. "It needs redecorating. I only moved in seven weeks ago, and I've been busy."

"I thought maybe you'd decided gold-foiled ceilings and

baroque furniture was your thing. Killer views, though. Get much use out of the craps table in your living room? Or that swimming pool on the patio?"

"No and yes. I see you found the wine."

"I did. Your taste in booze has obviously improved." She holds up her glass in mocking salute, then downs half the contents.

I smile and sip the cab. "Eat your dinner. I assume you still enjoy a good filet and baked potato?"

"That's never going to change."

She digs in and takes a bite. I watch as she shuts her eyes and savors the tender beef. A few things get to Eryn without fail. Good food and good sex are surefire winners. I intend to ply her with both tonight.

In the background, Ed Sheeran croons. Forks clink against dishes. Eryn swallows. Tension stretches thick between us.

"Did you sign the contract?" I ask.

"I brought it with me so we could discuss. You outlined quite a list of 'duties.' They're creative. Obviously, you've given this some thought."

"Does that surprise you?"

"The West I knew years ago was driven without being a prick about it. But hey, I should be glad there was no start-each-day-with-a-blow-job clause."

"Eryn, stop trying to push me into losing my temper. I won't fall for it, and you're only going to get more frustrated. You came here for a reason—"

"The money," she assures me with a raised brow before she downs more wine.

I don't believe her for a minute. In the past, she often misbehaved until she riled me so much I had to fuck her hard enough to put her in line. Is that what she wants now?

Barely tasting my food, I shovel in bites and examine the situation while I wait for her to finish.

"You know, when I locked Java and Jacks' door behind me today, two of my customers nearly cried."

"Your coffee is beyond buttery and smooth, so I understand. I'm sorry you have to close down. I know it's more than a mere inconvenience when you're building a business. If I had any way around the issue..."

Some of her prickly demeanor eases. "You didn't. I know because I called the city. The timing just sucks."

I can't argue with that. "How has business been since you took over?"

"It slumped at first. Some of the regulars were worried I wouldn't keep the same coffee and maintain the usual standards. But they've all come back now—and brought friends, so it's good." Her animated expression wanes. "I wish I'd known how tough running a restaurant was really going to be. I'm acclimating...slowly. You know I've always been a night owl, so being in bed by eight p.m. is a shock to my system and my social life."

I smile. "You would have been better off running a bar."

"Don't think I haven't thought of that..."

"What's stopping you? You've got the restaurant space and a prime location. Once the construction is done, it wouldn't take you long to morph the place into a hopping night spot."

Not that I want her to. I'm hoping at the end of six weeks,

she'll be ready to sell the place and move to Vegas for good. But for now, one step at a time.

She shrugs. "Actually, I've been wishing lately that I'd gone to college. I've waited tables my whole adult life, and I want to do something different. But Ella and I both knew Echo needed an education if she was going to be a physical therapist. By the way, she got married, you know? Ella, not Echo. To a great guy. Carson runs the Sweet Darlin' Candy Company. She moved with him to North Carolina recently."

"That's great for her. I love everything Sweet Darlin' makes. And Echo is almost done with school, so that's good."

"For a while, I thought about matriculating once she graduates, but now that I've got the restaurant..." Suddenly, she seems to remember that I'm the enemy, and her expression closes up. "I'll figure it out."

I add this new wrinkle to the list of considerations for our future. "You will. And I'm happy to be a sounding board if you want to talk."

"Nope. You know why I'm here."

"Money."

She nods. "That's it."

"And the sex."

"Not my first motivation, but it doesn't hurt."

Oh, that's a lie. Eryn has these little tells when she's being less than honest. One is that she can't keep a straight face, so I know she's absolutely here for the sex.

"Let's talk about the contract. I want that signed before anything commences."

"Not so fast. I want to negotiate."

This ought to be interesting. "Shoot."

"I want one day a week off."

"No." I refuse to give her time and space to build more fortifications against me.

"That's not a negotiation, West. That's a brick wall. You're not even hearing my argument."

"Fine. I'll listen, but you won't change my mind."

Eryn huffs, looking flustered. "You're so stubborn."

"Pot meet kettle."

She just rolls her eyes. "I want one night a week to gamble, see shows, or sight-see. I've only been here once. I hardly remember the trip."

I take a bite of steak and sit back to process what she's said. Once I swallow, I shake my head. "It's Vegas. You can gamble twenty-four seven. Feel free to hit the slots during the day. Same with sight-seeing. Shows are in the evenings, and if you want to go, I'll try to figure out a way to take you without being mobbed by the press."

"I'll want to go home, check on Echo and my apartment some weeks, too."

"I know you." I plant my elbows on the table and lean close, until we're inches apart. "You're wanting time away from me so you can remember all the reasons you should hate me without my touch clouding your thoughts. The answer is no. Next?"

She bristles. "You don't own me, Weston Quaid."

"I intend to for the next six weeks."

Silence. Eryn pushes her half-empty plate aside. "I can't do this. I'm going back to LA."

Since she doesn't move, I suspect it's an empty threat. She wants to see how far she can push me, if I'll cede any power to her. I will...but not until I'm sure she's actually giving us a chance.

"If you walk out the door, my offer is null and void. I hope you've got a better way to make money and explore one of the most exciting cities in the world, all while having the best sex of your life. If you do, don't let me stop you."

Eryn stands. I hold my breath, more than a little worried I've pushed her too far. Honestly, I'd rather wrap my arms around her, kiss her, take her to bed, and love her long into the night. But she's not ready for that yet, so I have to be patient—for now.

Instead of grabbing her suitcases and leaving my apartment, she strolls to the picture windows with a view of the Stratosphere in the distance. "You're a bastard, West."

"So you've said."

"Running a company has hardened you."

"It needed to if I was going to be successful and keep my job."

She cocks her head. "When we were dating, you said you didn't want that job."

"Things change. Do you want to hear the reasons? I'll be happy to tell you."

Eryn ignores my question. "I've changed, too. If you have any notion that you're going to find ways to make me fall in love with you again, that's not going to happen. You should tear up this silly contract, and we should go our separate ways."

I'll take my chances. "Thanks for the FYI."

Finally, she turns, arms crossed over her chest. "If you're not trying to wear my heart down again, why do you want me here?"

"My job is high stress. I want a mistress, not a hassle." On some level that's true, but it's a complete falsehood where she's concerned. But the lie will let her feel safe...and her guard will come down.

"I noticed the agreement prohibits me from dating anyone else. But you don't have to adhere to the same standard?"

I didn't include anything to that effect because I'm not interested in anyone else. But if adding that to the contract will make her feel as if she's won a negotiation point, fine. And it's a good sign that she's feeling a bit possessive.

Rising, I hold out my hand. "Give me the envelope. I'll make the amendment now."

"I'm not done." She turns, seemingly following the bank of windows into the living room.

It feels more like she's desperate to maintain distance.

"What else?"

"This naked-all-the-time thing is ridiculous. First, it's October, and the weather is getting colder. Second, I'm the kind of girl who *needs* a bra. Third, you didn't mention anything about dinner, but I can't cook in the buff without risking my skin. And I can't eat in the buff with you. I'll starve to death."

It's not easy, but I repress my smile. The truth is, I expected her to push back on this and I've already got a strategy. "You can keep the heater set at whatever temperature is comfortable for you. I'll find garments I approve of that support you"—*and your very lush breasts*—"adequately. I didn't ask you here to cook for me. It's not required, but if you're so inclined, I would appreciate it. I'll make sure you have the apron of your choice for such occasions. Eating *au naturel*... I'm afraid I can't bend on that point except to assure you that I won't let you starve."

"I'm not a toy, West."

She has no other argument, so I know I've won. I also notice that she didn't question my intentionally vague clause about eating dinner at the time and place of my choosing. Eryn will figure out soon enough that phrase has nothing to do with me choosing whether we eat dinner at seven in my apartment or at eight at a restaurant along the Strip.

"You're not," I assure her instead.

Silence. She wrings her hands and continues staring down from the windows, like she's cornered and looking for a way out.

"Eryn, I'll try to persuade you, maybe even push. But I can't force you to sign the contract, and we both know it."

"It's probably not even enforceable."

True, but after a lot of education and a couple of years of running an operation the size of Quaid Enterprises, I've learned the value of agreements. The tighter the better. "I merely wanted the lines and rules to be very clear between us."

Eryn taps a nervous thumb against her thigh, refusing to look my way. "But I don't see any boundaries in here for you. I can't disturb you at the office unless there's an emergency. I can't protest if you have to work late or on weekends. And I can't terminate this agreement without forfeiting every dime you owe me. Where are my protections?"

I'm impressed. She's driving a harder bargain than I

SHAYLA BLACK

anticipated. "You'll have your own bathroom. If you're in there, I'll keep out. If I violate your personal space, I'll owe you...say, a thousand dollars."

"Ten."

"Excuse me?"

"Ten thousand," she counters. "This contract is so slanted in your favor. There should be something that's weighted significantly in mine."

"The bathroom is for you to take care of your personal needs. It's not a safe space for you to hide. As long as you agree to the spirit of that interpretation, then fine. I'll pay you ten thousand dollars every time I violate your privacy."

"You should prorate my 'service.'"

I raise a brow. "Meaning?"

Finally, she turns to me, and I see the argument all over her face. She's stalling. She's afraid of what comes next.

I soften.

"Well..." She swallows. "Like any job, if I work two weeks, then quit, I get paid for the time I spent in that position."

So she's looking for the early-out clause. Maybe she's calculated exactly how much money she needs to scrape by while Java and Jacks is closed and intends to stay only for that long—not a minute more.

"You're a contractor, not an employee. You earn by the project, not by the hour. I'll pay you when the job is done."

Her mouth twists into a scowl. "Maybe you should pay me by the orgasm."

Now she's hitting low. Because she's feeling powerless? Because she's itching for a fight? Either way, I can't let this

75

point of contention go. I'm not even sure six weeks will be enough to win her back, so I can't negotiate anything that would potentially afford her to leave sooner.

"This isn't just about the sex, Eryn." I stroll closer, slowly, giving her time to flee. "It's about your company, too. If it makes you feel better to know that I've missed you over the last three years and regret the fact we weren't able to spend that time together, I'll admit that. But I refuse to compensate you by the sex act. As you so aptly pointed out when I first propositioned you, you're not a whore. Any more objections?"

She presses her lips together. "It says in the agreement that you require a minimum of an hour's conversation a day. Does that include the conversation during dinner?"

"If you'd like."

"I would. I'd also like you to clarify what you mean by 'presentable' when we go out."

"Dressed both appropriately for the occasion and to my liking."

"So I can spend time getting ready, and you alone have the power to say it's not okay and that I have to start over?"

"If you prefer, we can discuss everything in advance to avoid a waste of time and energy." Finally, I close the distance between us. "I think you're dreaming up objections to avoid what happens next. I want you, Eryn. I've made no secret of that. I'll amend the contract as we've discussed, but once that's done and we've signed, I expect you to start abiding by the agreement."

"By taking off my clothes, getting into your bed, and spreading my legs?"

"If that's what I want, yes."

She turns her back on me. "You really are a bastard."

I smile grimly. I knew winning her back would be an uphill battle...but I'm making progress. "Are you signing or not?"

"Where's my luggage?"

"In my bedroom."

She rolls her eyes. "Of course it is. Wait here."

I have zero intention of doing any such thing. Instead, I follow her down the hall and into the master suite. Though the beige tones are neutral, the decor itself is incredibly gaudy. I don't really need 6,400 square feet to myself, and my clothes could never take up all the space in the enormous closet. But the views in this high-rise condo are unparalleled. I have panoramic views of the Strip from my patio. This penthouse simply needs a cosmetic overhaul before it will feel like home.

"Why am I not surprised you're following me?" she mutters. "And why does that massive-ass bed look like a million flamboyantly kinky fantasies might have been fulfilled here?"

"You're still stalling."

Eryn sighs as she digs into one of her bags and produces the envelope and pen I left with her. "Whatever. Here you go."

"Excuse me." I head toward my home office.

Ten minutes. That's how long I'm going to be forced to clamp down on my anticipation to make the requisite changes.

"I'm drinking more wine," she calls after me. "Did you order dessert?"

"In the fridge." I shout back.

She might not admit how excited she is when she opens the container, but when she puts a bite of the smooth chocolate panna cotta layered with banana ricotta cookies in her mouth, she's going to flip. That woman loves dessert. And she especially loves chocolate.

As much as it chafes, I hole myself in my office long enough to draft the changes we discussed. I call my attorney for confirmation. I pay him to be available to me day or night. Luckily, he doesn't keep me waiting. The moment he's perfected the changes, he emails me a new document. I notice my hands tremble as I pull it off the printer, sign it, and fold it into a crisp new envelope.

Heaving a sigh, I stand and find Eryn back in the dining room, glass of cab in one hand, fork in the other, making orgasmic sounds that leave me aching as she savors her dessert.

"I thought you might like that," I murmur.

"You play underhanded, Quaid."

Something I'm sure she'll utter more than once before she finally realizes that everything I've done has been designed not to take advantage of her but to get us back together.

Instead, I toss the envelope on the table in front of her. "Changes made. I've signed." Gently, I set the pen on the table beside her plate. "Your turn."

Eryn peers up at me. "Once I do, how long will it be before you penetrate me?"

"Three minutes. Maybe less."

"Hmm." She peers down at her plate. "I think I'll consider this matter a bit more while I finish my dessert."

"Don't toy with me." My patience is already wearing thin.

Her answering smile is full of challenge. "Or what?"

"Sign it now. Or you'll find out."

CHAPTER FIVE

ERYN

I distract myself by taking another bite of the heavenly dessert and let the flavor linger on my tongue. But I can't seem to pry my stare off West.

Stalling is only postponing the inevitable. I came here for the sex. The money is a super-helpful side benefit, but I'm here to screw him out of my system. He probably has some inkling of that. The question is, how should I handle him? I don't want to seem too eager or too desperate. I certainly don't want to make this easy on him. I've got walls between us; I need to be completely certain they're in place before I let him any closer. I can't risk him prying me open. I can't put my heart on the line with this man again.

Slowly, I walk my fingers across his dining room table. Well, not his. He must have bought this unit furnished, because absolutely nothing here fits his taste. It really does look like a drag queen's fantasy pad, complete with overlarge crystal chandelier. I don't see an ounce of masculine simplicity anywhere.

Finally, I open the envelope and extract the revised contract, then pick up the pen and scan his verbiage changes, which he's helpfully underlined. Phrasing he's eliminated has been stricken-through. He's even initialed all the changes and signed the last page. All I have to do is put my signature next to his.

As I swallow the last bite of dessert and pretend I'm still reading, I breathe through the excitement scorching my veins. I can literally feel his desire. It hangs in the air, scented like musk and testosterone, sharpening the moment. It blends with my own thrill and fills me with an anticipation I can barely stand.

Just to keep him dangling, I set everything down, then lift our used plates from the table and take them to the sink. I don't rush as I rinse them off and open the dishwasher.

"Eryn..." He raises a brow at me. "Last warning."

"Don't I get a minute to consider? Don't you want dinner cleared from this...ahem, lovely table?"

"You had all weekend and another five hours in the car to consider. You already decided to come here, and you know why. You stalling now is merely for spite."

"How do you figure that?"

"You know every minute you're making me wait is torment."

I do know, and I give him the accompanying smile. "Really?"

West grits his teeth. "If you couldn't tell from my demeanor, fine. I admit it; you're killing me. Now sign."

Once I do, I'll lose all control of the situation. We both know it. I'm in no rush—or I try not to be. But his lust and his impatience are driving my own. I hate that I'm already pinging with need for him. I hate that I only have to look at him to ache. I hate that I already know he's going to overwhelm me with pleasure, and that, if I don't keep my wits about me, I'll surrender my soul.

And I know I'll love his every touch.

After all, Weston Quaid is like a shark. He'll smile as he's consuming me.

"You know..." I drawl as I finish loading the plates in the dishwasher. "It was a long day on the road. If we're going to do this, I should be at my freshest. I think I should shower."

"You don't need to clean up so I can get you dirty," he bites out, then grabs the agreement and the pen off the table and slams them on the bar in front of me. "You have ten seconds to sign, or I'm going to come over there and wring a screaming yes out of you that every one of my neighbors will hear."

Normally, that wouldn't be a threat. If any other man said those words to me, I would pray he could give me the kind of ecstasy to make it true. But this is West. He *can* make me scream. He can also make me pant, whimper, and beg while he's undoing me completely.

Why am I egging him on?

Because some subversive part of my brain loves feeling my feminine power and knowing his retribution is going to feel so, so good.

Swallowing, I reach for the paper and the pen. My hands shake as I fumble for the last page.

I have no other objections—or better options. Sure, I could be mad at him for backing me into this corner. But I could have said no. I'm not afraid of hard work. I could have figured out how to make ends meet other than in West's bed. But then I would have missed out on this. On him.

The truth is, I want him and I want pleasure. I just need to own up to that and sign.

"Ten. Nine. Eight—"

"You're impatient."

"Yes, and I'm done with your stalling. Five. Four."

The devil on my shoulder still can't resist needling him. "I'm not sure this pen is working…"

He grabs it from my grip and tests the ballpoint on the envelope. His scrawl appears in bold black, and he scowls at me. "Three. Two. On—"

I pluck the pen from his hand and jot my signature on the page, then shove both in his direction. "Happy?"

West spares a fraction of a second to ensure I actually signed on the dotted line, then he rounds the bar and prowls through the kitchen toward me, barreling as if nothing and no one will stop him from getting me naked and under him sooner than now.

I shiver. My sex clenches. He's staring at me with a driving hunger that makes my skin tingle and my heart thud.

I haven't felt anything close to this kind of dizzying thrill in three terrible years.

"West…" I back up, not even sure why. I want him, but I also love the chase. So does he. I've always loved driving him crazy.

He lunges for me and catches my wrists in his sturdy grip, then tugs me closer. Suddenly, he anchors his fist in my hair and crushes his body against mine. His intent—and his erection—are impossible to miss. "I warned you."

My breathing ramps up. The ache between my legs intensifies. "I'm not afraid of you."

"Good. I don't want you afraid. I want you hot, wet, and willing. I want your entire body pleasantly boneless and tender tomorrow. And while I'm at the office, I want you to feel me everywhere on you. In you. I was willing to start slow, Eryn, but you pushed me—"

"Bullshit. No matter what happened, the minute I signed you were going to drag me to your bed."

"Maybe. But now I'm going to make damn sure I wring every ounce of response out of you. By tomorrow, you will know you belong to me."

His words send warning bells through me. "Only for six weeks. Don't count on a second longer than that."

This time I don't mean to challenge him. I simply can't afford to relinquish anything but my body to West for a minute longer than our agreement. I'm already a bit afraid that I taunted him too much. And that now I'll pay the price.

The smile he sends me is dark and smug, full of a confidence that has my nipples beading and my heart leaping.

"Whatever you say, honey. Bedroom. Now."

West doesn't even give me the opportunity to get there on my own two feet. He bends and scoops me up against his chest, then strides down the hall so quickly that my peripheral vision is a blur.

"I can walk!"

"Not fast enough. This way, I'll be sure I get you there and get you naked before I lose my sanity." As if to punctuate his statement, we're suddenly in the middle of the master suite way faster than I would have thought possible. Before I can even process his insistence, he releases me, letting every inch of my body slide down his. Then he bends and tears off my athletic shoes. "Lose the shirt."

I bite my lip, holding in a protest. Everything is happening so quickly. I'm still blinking as he reaches for the drawstring of my athletic pants.

"Now," he bites out.

I swallow. My skin crackles with electric desire. I want this. But I'm afraid.

West alone has the power to hurt me. Because I never got over him. As he's dragging my pants down and kissing his way up my belly toward my lips is a terrible time to finally acknowledge that.

Then the pleasure of his rough hands and hot mouth mapping my body overtakes me. He's everywhere, touching every place I've secretly needed it, arousing me in ways I swear no other man can.

"West..."

"I know, honey," he says as he tears off his casual Sunday T-shirt to expose his lean, rippled torso.

I'm not even conscious of what I'm doing. One moment I'm letting him take off my clothes. The next my hands and lips are roaming all over the flesh I haven't touched in far too long. I can't get enough of the velvety skin over the steel of his muscles. I need more of his salt, of his musk that rises from every place that makes him a man.

Two minutes in, and I feel weak-kneed, dizzy, and frantic.

He grips my shoulders and pries me off him for a torturous moment. "Take your shirt off."

On autopilot, I nod, then reach for the hem. With a tug, it's gone, and I toss it somewhere across the room. He can take care of the bra. I need to press myself against him, drag my tongue up the strong column of his neck, sniff in more of his scent that's addicting me again.

As I lift my thigh over his hip, he catches it and holds it in place, fitting his cock right against every aching nerve that's screaming out for him. With his free hand, he manages to unclasp my bra—he's still got that one-handed thing down to a science—and suddenly the scrap of wires and lace slumps between us. With two economical sweeps of his hand, the straps fall from my shoulders and he flings it away.

Now I'm clad in only a thong. My heart careens against my chest when I realize he's backed away enough to stare between my legs—at the damp spot darkening the champagne silk.

He swallows. "I want those underwear gone. I want my mouth on you again."

"Will you let me come this time?"

His answer doesn't come right away. Finally, he shakes his head. "The first orgasm I give you, I'll be buried deep inside you. You'll be feeling every inch of me. And I won't let you escape the knowledge that *I'm* the one giving you ecstasy."

My righteous protest withers under his words. Suddenly, breathing is beyond difficult, and I'm so light-headed that I'm swooning back onto the bed.

West follows me down, tearing into his zipper and kicking his jeans away. Then he's naked, his cock standing tall and insistent in the golden glow of the accent lights on the nightstands. As my back hits his thick brocade comforter, he tears off my delicate panties and starts kissing his way up my thighs.

I'm aching and writhing under him when he suddenly stops. "You still have this landing strip I told you to lose."

In the heat and the rush, I forgot about my silent fuck-you. Now, I fight to hold in a plea and an apology. Yes, I want West to understand that he can't have everything he wants just because he wants it. Now, more than ever, I need him to understand that. But will he really withhold pleasure?

"It's my body."

He gnashes his teeth together with a curse. "Why are you objecting now, Eryn? You never did in the past."

"Maybe I've decided that I mind." But I don't, not really. I don't know what's prodding me to defy him. History has shown that he's definitely going to give me more orgasms than I can handle. The only reason for my refusal now is my desire to control *something* between us, no matter how meaningless.

"What would you do in my shoes?" he surprises me by asking.

"Let it go."

He laughs. "No, you wouldn't. I know you too well."

I can't refute him when he's right. So I say nothing.

"You're supposed to groom the way I want you to. It's in the contract."

That raises my alarm. "It's not!"

"Oh, it is. Paragraph three, subparagraph six, clause B. You're to be presentable to my satisfaction."

SHAYLA BLACK

"When we go out." I'm positive that's what I read. Well, almost...

West shakes his head. "I wrote three-quarters of it myself. I know exactly what it says."

"*You* wrote most of that?"

He nods. "After I went home, I managed to finish my last semester of college at Columbia, then attended law school. While working as Quaid's CEO."

I blink. "*You* went to law school?"

"There's a lot you don't know about the last three years."

"Whose fault is that?"

His face shutters closed as he reaches into his jeans for his cell. "I'm done arguing about this."

With a puzzled frown, I watch as he sends a quick text. Almost immediately, he receives a reply. Then he smiles and tosses the device onto the nearest nightstand. "In the spa downstairs, Leona will clear up that landing strip at ten a.m. tomorrow."

On one level, it's heady that he cares about the state of my flesh he intends to use. On the other hand, I don't understand his insistence to have me bare. "Why are you trying so damn hard to control everything, even the state of my pubic hair?"

"Because I want back the sexual compatibility we once had. I want the naked dinners and the lazy Sunday afternoons. I want the long, hot nights of lovemaking. I want—" He lets out a rough breath and shakes his head. "I want your pussy bare."

That's not the whole truth. I know West's expressions too well. Oh, he wants to recreate something about our past. The question is why? And how much? But I'm guessing it's not just the sex. Holy cow, is he looking to make me his girlfriend? His "fiancée" again? Maybe...but now that I'm thinking about it, two and two aren't adding up.

Would he go to this much trouble simply to patch together a temporary relationship?

I stare at him, trembling. Does he think he's finally going to make me his wife? Or is that my maudlin heart wishing out loud?

More confused than ever, I finally nod. "All right. Whatever."

"You're not going to fight me on this anymore?"

Not until I figure out what's going on and what he's really after.

I shrug. "It's only hair. So I'm bare temporarily. If I don't like it, it will grow back."

His displeasure is subtle, but I notice his jaw tense. Yeah, now I'm really pondering his motivations and his mood that I clearly misjudged while I was too blinded by my own lust and bitterness, and too busy yanking his chain to see.

Suddenly, my heart is racing for a totally different reason.

I totally failed to notice his intent to win me back. And I'm in way over my head.

WEST

The sight of Eryn spread across my bed is one I've imagined a thousand times. To actually see her here, glowing under the lights on the bedside tables, looking both nervous and flushed, arouses me nearly past my restraint. I want to lay my body over hers, thrust deep, and mark her—then repeat the process over and over until she admits she's mine.

I can't. She'll give me her body, sure. But I'm after all of her—arms, legs, passion, heart—all the way down to the woman under her skin. I need her to surrender to us, let go of the pain she felt when I left and the anger she's been holding on to since, embrace that deep-down yearning she's felt to have us together that she doesn't want to admit.

Now that she's finally signed the agreement, I have time to make that happen.

That's one reason I'm insisting on her naked body and her naked pussy. Admittedly, I like her that way. Not gonna lie. But years ago, Eryn was very good at making me feel as if she was with me every moment in our relationship...then insecurity would rear its head. Her trust would suddenly evaporate until I could coax her back.

Once I met her parents, I understood her knee-jerk behavior. Her father is an investigative journalist first. Being a dad has always come in a very distant second. He actually left our celebratory engagement dinner to chase a story. Her mother stayed long enough to pay for our meals that night. Then she left with a distracted smile to finish a costume for a movie shooting the following week. They've always been lost in their careers, abandoning Eryn and her sisters to fend for themselves. I hate that for her.

Of course, my family is hardly ideal. I learned the hard way that, except for my siblings, they all have an agenda that has nothing to do with closeness or harmony. So I steer clear. After all, who wants to cozy up to a pit of vipers?

But that leaves me in a difficult place with Eryn, trying

to repair the damage that my dramatic and unexplained departure on our wedding day wrought. In one morning, I obliterated every bit of the trust she worked like hell to give me. At the time, doing damage control was most critical. I thought I'd have time to return, to explain, to patch everything back together and spend my life with her.

I was wrong.

"West?"

Eryn's hesitant voice brings me back to the present. She's naked. I'm naked. I can't dwell on the past now. I have to look forward and fight for our future.

I lower myself onto the bed, pressing against her. "Sorry. Just thinking about all the delicious ways I'm going to make you scream."

She frowns. "Good. For a minute, you looked...sad."

Would she care to know I have been without her? Probably not yet.

I try my best to laugh off her observation. "When I've got you here and in my bed?"

To abort the question I see in her expression, I nuzzle her neck and nip at her lobe, letting my hands roam her body, fingers grazing the curve of her breasts before skimming her softness, playing in her naval, then traveling south again. As I wander closer to her sex, she holds her breath. Her hips wriggle. Her exhalations become little whimpers.

"We should...um, talk birth control," she manages to murmur.

A decidedly unromantic topic. Plus, once we're married, it's not something I want to control much. I'd love to have three or four kids with Eryn. She might be skittish in relationships, but she's great with children. That surprised me, but I've seen her in action. She loves them unconditionally.

"I'm clean," I murmur against her shoulder before I nibble her smooth skin. "I have a recent physical to prove it."

Her breath catches. "I am, too. But...I'm not on the pill anymore."

This evening just keeps getting better and better. Her admission tells me she hasn't been with many guys since our split. And we're in the quickie marriage capital of the world, so if I'm able to sweet-talk her to the altar...maybe it won't be too long before she's in maternity clothes. Yes, I'm rushing, and I know we have to make these decisions together. But I'm eager to tie her to me in every way. If Eryn had been my wife these last three years, we'd probably already be parents. I'm dying to make up for lost time.

"So I brought condoms," she adds into the silence.

Of course she did. Eryn is always both practical and prepared. Logically, I know we shouldn't even think about having a baby until we repair our relationship. But I want more. I want all of her now.

"Let's make sure we put them to good use, then."

If I'm going to have a tomorrow with Eryn, I have to curb my impatience and start unraveling her. Making love to her is no hardship, so that's what I plan to do. She's expecting me to fuck her. To use her. I know she plans to do the same to me. I understand. And maybe she's after a little revenge, too. In her mind, I've earned it.

Hopefully, that will change once I explain that every

choice I made in the past was purely to protect her.

I roll onto Eryn, pinning her to the bed with my body weight, then lace our fingers together and spread her arms wide. I push her legs apart with my own and shower her with kisses. On her forehead. Against her temple. Down her cheeks. I'm in no hurry and have no particular destination.

Immediately, she chafes, trying to rise beneath me and meld our mouths together. Clearly, she has an it's-just-sex agenda. I'm not playing along.

"Patience..." I chide.

"If three years wasn't a long enough wait for you, we can put this off until tomorrow."

I tamp down a smile. "I warned you what would happen if you teased me. You didn't listen."

Under me, she stills. "So now you're going to tease me in return?"

My smile widens. "You're getting the idea."

"West, that's not..." She shakes her head. "Never mind."

"Fair? Nowhere in our agreement did it state that I had to play fair. I own you until six a.m. I can please, tease, pleasure, or torment you however I want. Remember?"

Right now, I want to make the love we're sharing last forever.

"Whatever."

She says the word dismissively, but her body tells me something else entirely. Beneath me, she's restless. Her skin burns fever-hot. I can smell her damp musk rising between us, driving me absolutely mad.

I brush her smooth cheek with my stubbled one. "I've missed you."

"You don't have to say anything romantic. The lies are a waste of your breath."

"Lies always are." Stifling my irritation, I press my lips to her ear. "I mean every word of this. I've missed you, honey. More than you know."

Beneath me, she spreads her thighs wider, bends her knees, and cradles my hips. Suddenly, I'm prodding her slick opening, and she lifts, inviting me in. "Shh. Condoms are in the purple makeup case on the dresser."

"Thank you. I'll remember that when I need one... eventually."

Her huff of frustration is adorable. "What do you want, West?"

"For you to hush and let me make you feel good."

Being silent goes against Eryn's grain. But thankfully, she stops arguing. I reward her with a string of kisses down her cheek, a brush of my tongue over her bottom lip. As I enjoy the flavor of her skin, she fits perfectly against me. It's all I can do not to melt into her.

While I lave her neck, she shivers, gasping as I scrape my teeth over that stubborn pointed chin, then work my way back to her mouth. Next, I lay my lips over hers softly, reverently, little more than a brush. I pull back, hover, make her wait.

At first she doesn't take the bait, so I repeat the cycle a few times until finally she sighs against me and rears up, trying to fuse our mouths together. I don't capitulate right away, merely sweep my lips across hers once more.

"West..." she pleads when I ease back.

There. Now she's with me, starting to want more than just sex.

I prop myself on my elbows and peer down into her face. "Want to hear something else that's not a lie? I've missed you more than I ever thought possible."

She opens her mouth to protest, but I swoop in and take control of our kiss, heaping sensations on her. My tongue glides along hers as I gather a fistful of her soft curls in my hands. She jolts and opens wider, urging me deeper, silently telling me that she's done playing games...for now.

Later, I'll deal with whatever she schemes up. For the moment, I kiss her until her breathing turns heavy, until our pants mingle and she's clinging to me as if she's waited forever for this. Then I skim my lips down her jaw and work my way toward her breasts.

I haven't forgotten my way around Eryn's body. She loves me at her nipples. Sure, she enjoys it when I'm tender with them. But she goes insane with lust when I get rough. The merciless stimulation never failed to make her want and beg in the past. I'm hoping like hell nothing has changed.

Cradling her breasts in my hands, I bend to brush a gossamer kiss across them, one after the other, dragging my lips up the swells, grazing the tips, then sliding into the soft, scented valley between. In my head, I know Eryn is put together like most other women—two eyes, two lips, two breasts, two hips, two legs. But somehow, with her, everything feels different.

Guess that's being in love.

Eryn reaches between us and pinches her nipples. I grab her wrists and tug her hands away.

"Those are mine to play with," I remind.

"You don't seem all that interested."

"I'm getting there. Were you trying to make them harder to entice me or stimulate yourself for the hell of it?"

"Either works."

I would think she's being flippant except I hear the breathy whine of need in her voice. My slow seduction is getting to her.

"I'll take it from here," I assure her.

She blinks up at me, her face full of challenge. "What if I'm not convinced?"

Resist? Or fall into her trap? No contest. Giving her what she wants right now makes us both feel damn good.

"Let's see what I can do," I murmur as I dip my head to stroke one hard bud with my tongue.

Her body jerks. Her breath catches. Between my lips, the sweet buds harden even more.

I pull on one, deep and long, pursing my mouth around the tip, gratified when she twists with a needy groan under me.

"More."

"Tell me."

"You don't remember? Of course you don't." She gives me an irritated push.

I smile through her short, hot breaths and hold her in place. I know exactly what she wants. Still, I make her wait, drawing out her anticipation. "Is that what you think?"

"I don't care. Just...do whatever you're going to do."

"Look at me." I refuse to move a muscle until she complies. "When it comes to you, I've forgotten nothing."

Eryn is still forming a flippant comeback when I sink my teeth into her tender tips. Gently, at first. A mere hint of a nip. A little scrape. Then, just when she thinks I'm going to pull back, I apply more pressure.

She hisses in pleasure and tries to lift her hands from the bed, presumably to direct my movements. I keep her pinned below me, my fingers firm vises around her wrists, holding her in place.

"I remember. And you don't want to go anywhere." I dare her to refute me.

"I never said I did, but—"

"And you'll get plenty of opportunity to touch me soon."

"But—"

"Stop arguing. You aren't going to change the way I make love to you or the speed at which I do it."

Her mouth takes on a mutinous pout. "We're just fucking."

"Keep telling yourself that."

Her eyes widen. "If you brought me out here for some romantic reunion—"

"You're my mistress. You signed an agreement to that effect. I expect you to live up to your end of the bargain."

"I will when you do," she counters, lifting her hips under me, gliding the head of my cock through her slick folds. "All you have to do is slide inside me."

"Did you forget the part where you serve at my pleasure? That's whatever I want, Eryn." I grab her chin. "Stop trying to control this."

She's doing her best not to feel anything for me—and I'm determined she will. I'm also done talking, so I slant my mouth over hers and delve so deep, she has no choice but to quiet down and take me. I stay. I stroke. I seduce. Little by little, the tension begins to melt from Eryn's body. Her breaths soften, just like her lips. Under me, she arches again, invites me closer, inching toward surrender.

But if I don't heap bliss on Eryn quickly, her head will kick in and the pushback will start once more. Yes, she's afraid. I take that as a good sign. If she felt nothing for me, she'd be happy to go through the motions. The woman beneath me is fighting her response because I get to her. Because she's not sure she can stop herself from wanting—or falling for—me in return.

This time, I don't make the fatal mistake of talking as I kiss my way down to her breasts. Instead, I wrap my mouth around her tempting mounds and suck the tips ruthlessly, back and forth, giving her pleasure an edge with a gentle bite of my teeth. It's too soon to start celebrating when she sucks in a sharp inhalation and fidgets restlessly. I'm on my way to making her putty in my hands, but I still have plenty of her defenses to tear down. So I shift breasts again, inhaling one against the roof of my mouth as I give the other a savage pinch.

This time, she jolts. Her breath stutters. A whimper escapes her.

I remember exactly what she likes—and I'm happy to prove it.

Back and forth, I swap the tips in my mouth, relishing the way they harden and swell. I could do this all day—and at some point, I will—but it's been so long since I've been inside her. I'm desperate to start claiming her again.

When I lift my head to survey her reaction, I see her nipples are no longer a rosy-brown but a sweetly flushed red. I have no idea how much time has passed, but Eryn doesn't have any more sass at the moment, just ragged breaths as she digs her fingers into my arms in a silent plea.

I brush my thumbs over the distended tips. "More?"

When she lifts her lids to look at me, she's glassy-eyed, aroused. "They're sore and tight."

"That's not what I asked. Do you want more, honey?"

With her defenses weakening, I see her weighing whether she should risk asking for something she knows will arouse her or taking the safe road and insisting I simply put out her fire. "I want you inside me."

She does...but she's still thinking more than she should.

"Yeah?" I pinch the tender nubs again, then give them a brisk tug.

Eryn shudders and moans, reaching for me again.

I pin her wrists to the mattress once more and dip my head to breathe across her nipples. "I think you want more of my mouth on you. I think you need it."

The moment I lave one, she tenses as if she's bracing against the sensation. I won't have that, so I suction the swollen flesh into my mouth with a hearty pull before slowly releasing her breast, nipping my way down the protruding tip. She jerks and keens, digging her nails into my hands. Because she can't take any more? Or because she's dying for me to continue?

Easing back, I study her rosy face, her short breaths, her unfocused gaze.

Seconds become a minute as I catalog every facet of her reaction. In this moment, she isn't pushing me away or demanding that I let her go. Nope. She's arching up to me in silent plea.

SHAYLA BLACK

"I need it," she finally whispers. "I've needed it for so long."

"Why?" I demand, kissing my way around her sensitive nipples, coming close...but not quite touching them.

"No one knows my body like you."

Triumph spikes my bloodstream. "No one ever will, Eryn. Think about that while I make you feel good."

I dip to heap more sensations on her aching twin tips. A lick, a nip, a moment of deep suction followed by a teasing touch. I watch her every reaction as I work both of her breasts, loving every twist and hiss and scratch she gives me in return.

"Please," Eryn pants. "Please... I'm dying."

Finally, she's reached that delicate peak where stimulation is about to become pain. Right here is where arousal overwhelms her. *Now* she'll give me anything and everything I want—especially herself.

With a smile, I bolt up from the mattress and find the condoms in her bag, tearing the box open and taking one plastic-wrapped prophylactic off the chain. I sidle up to her and ease the condom onto her belly, then glide my fingers through her oh-so-swollen pussy with a groan. "Oh, honey..."

"West!" She writhes and roots, urging me to fill the chasm of her ache.

I settle my fingers over her clit and lick my way up the side of her breast. "Soon."

"Now!"

Not quite. I know how far I can push her. I know where instinct takes over and need drowns out her insecurities. "A little longer. I have to touch you."

When I start rubbing her most nerve-laden spot, she

shrieks and thrashes, throwing her hips up at me. "Enough!"

I hold her down. "It's enough when I say it's enough."

Her whimper sounds like a protest, but I know Eryn loves it when I drive her past coherence.

I rub her again, this time in slow, torturous circles that I know damn well are only honing her ache into an agony that's bringing her close to her euphoric breaking point.

Eryn digs her heels into the mattress. Beneath my fingers, I feel her clit swell and harden. She holds her breath, begins to twitch.

"West!" Her shrill, almost incoherent voice tells me she's going to melt down if I don't let her come.

Now she's exactly where I want her.

I lift my fingers from her flesh, grab the condom, annoyed that my own hands are shaking, then tear the package open. Thank god the little ring of rubber rolls quickly down my cock.

My gorgeous ex is still crying out in protest as I shove her to the middle of the bed, vault between her outstretched thighs, then surge inside her deep, filling her in one breath-stealing stroke.

As her swollen flesh closes around me, a groan rips from my chest. I haven't been a monk since Eryn, but no one—no matter how much I wished otherwise—feels half as good as this woman.

"Oh, that's so fucking good," I rasp in her ear.

Beneath me, she tosses her head back and keens. Seeing her—wrists restrained by my grip, hips held immobile by my own—is a sight I've dreamed of a million times in the last three years. The fact it's real only jacks my desire up another thousandfold.

"Hurry..." she demands.

I shake my head. "You're not controlling this."

"Why are you?"

"Because I know what I need. I know what you need, too."

To prove my point, I roll to my back, taking her with me until she's straddling my hips and gravity drives my cock deeper. Eryn gasps at this new ripple of pleasure, but I don't give her a moment to acclimate. Immediately, I pull her against my chest, take her lips, and rise up beneath her in driving strokes, hitting that one perfect spot over and over...

She wrenches free. "*West!*"

Eryn's brain might tell her to resist surrendering, but her body won't allow it. Above me, she writhes as she slams down onto my waiting erection, meeting me thrust for thrust as she claws the sheets and howls through a shattering climax.

It's the most fucking perfect moment.

"That's it. Come for me. Yeah... Oh, honey. Fuck, you're pretty. More..."

With a tight grip on her hips, I guide her through the pinnacle of her orgasm, then help her glide back down until she's a panting heap on my chest.

I try to focus on stroking her back until she falls to earth again, but she feels so perfect pressed against me, all around me. As if my hands have a will of their own, my palms skate down her spine until each has a handful of her ass. Then I'm lifting into her again, each thrust quicker and more insistent than the last.

Half a dozen in, she tenses above me.

"West?" Her voice shakes.

In that one word, I hear her silent question: how is it possible her body is already reawakening and aching for me again?

I can't reply to the question that has no logical answer. It simply is.

"I'm here." I murmur the words against her neck, dragging my lips up her jaw.

Mentally, I whoop out a glory fucking hallelujah when she turns her head and presses her mouth over mine. Then our lips meld, our breaths merge, our tongues tangle. God, I don't know how much longer I can stave off this need to release inside her. But I need to try long enough to send her tailspinning into rapture once more.

I throw her onto her back, grip her hips. One after the other, I hammer out deep, relentless strokes. Under me, Eryn grips me with her thighs, rocks with me, and digs her nails into my back.

"It's building so fast..." she mutters.

"Yeah." As I shove my way deeper, I grip her hair in my fist and give it a little tug until our stares collide. "There's no one like you, Eryn."

She closes her eyes between us. I'm half expecting pushback or an argument. Instead, a fresh flush crawls up her body. She begins to tighten up. Her breathing stutters. Her nails leave ten points of fire in my back that only drives my desire hotter.

When she clamps down on me and wails, her entire body seizing with pleasure, I fucking lose it. The brewing tingles gather and thicken. The pressure crescendos into a towering desire that threatens to flatten me. Oh, it will be the most amazing orgasm ever—I can already tell—but it's going to exhaust my body, fuck with my head, and totally wreck my heart.

I can't make myself care about any of that.

"Eryn!" Her name is the only word I can get past my lips as I pump her harder, deeper, and the blinding euphoria explodes me into a million tiny irreparable pieces.

Frantically, I pummel my way from rise to peak, then ride her through the most deliciously slow, toe-curling descent to a shuddering, replete stop.

When it's over, I collapse on top of Eryn. The only part of me that's moving now is my chest, which is rapidly rising and falling with the frantic beat of my heart and the filling of my overtaxed lungs.

What. The. Fuck. Just. Happened?

Almost instantly, Eryn shoves at me frantically, whimpering and jerking like a wild thing. Frowning, I force my sated body to withdraw from her snug clasp and roll aside.

"What's wrong?" Maybe I'm too heavy and she can't breathe.

The second she's free, she lurches off the bed and darts toward the *hers* bathroom on the far side of the master suite—the one place I've vowed not to violate her privacy.

I'm barely on my feet by the time she's gripping the door. Tears stream down her face. Her dark eyes accuse me. "Don't ever do that again!"

Make her feel. That's what she means. And my heart sinks as she slams the door between us, then locks it. Fuck. Nothing else could say more emphatically that she's throwing walls up between us again.

Her sobs on the other side tear at my heart. I remember the last time I heard her cry—the morning we didn't get married. I know she's hurting, and I feel helpless to stop it. But I'll fucking try because three years ago, I let the situation dictate my behavior and, therefore, the outcome. This time, I give zero fucks about playing by the rules. I'm going to make that woman mine.

CHAPTER SIX

ERYN

I lean against the door, palm pressing against my chest, as if I can somehow keep my heart from escaping its chamber and attaching itself again to Weston Quaid.

Tears fall. He's seen them. I hate that. I also hate that, where he's concerned, I'm weak.

For nearly three years, I've been utterly single. Since then, I congratulated myself every time I hooked up with a guy and felt nothing. I was over West, and I was *so* beyond that blooming-love shit. Never again would I be vulnerable to another man. I was untouchable, invincible. Unconquerable.

A few hours with West has proven me devastatingly wrong.

Sure, I knew my body responded to him. He's hot. He's always been good in bed. I expected orgasm-central.

I didn't expect him to affect more than my vagina.

Knowing he touched me much deeper is bitterly disappointing.

"Eryn, honey..." West calls from the other side of the door.

Even the sound of his voice wrenches my chest and dredges up fresh sobs. "Go away."

"I'm never going to do that." I hear him sigh. "Not again."

Everything in his voice tells me to believe him. I'm annoyed by how badly my heart wants to. My head relays another message entirely, one I wish I'd heeded when I first met him: *He's not for you. He's better than you. He'll never love you.*

But like an idiot, I let myself believe back then.

Eventually, I forgave myself for being young, gullible—and okay—overwhelmed by the amazing sex. But I know that old saying: Fool me once, shame on you. Fool me twice...

There will be no shaming me again.

I need to get my shit under control. And I need to plan ahead so that next time West touches me, I'm not blindsided by all these unresolved feelings.

I drag in a shuddering breath and will my tears away. Carefully, I craft a reply, intentionally misunderstanding what he said. "I'm fine. Don't worry. Today was just a long day. I need a shower and some sleep. Tomorrow you'll see a whole new me."

To head off any further discussion, I flip on the shower in the giant walk-in. While the water heats up, I grab a tissue off the vanity, staring at my mottled cheeks and red-rimmed eyes. *Hell no.* When Weston Quaid sets eyes on me again, I'm going to be cool and collected.

After blowing my nose, I step under the hot spray. I ribbed West about the decor of this place because most of it is hideously overdone. But the bones of the penthouse—and this bathroom—are the stuff of fantasy. The views from nearly every room are stunning. The ceilings are interesting, either coved or coffered. If the carpet was replaced, the furniture swapped out for something simpler, the ornamentation stripped, and the wall treatments scaled back for simple paint, this place would be ideal—for entertaining, for living, for enjoying family. Even for raising kids.

Was he thinking of any of those things when he bought a penthouse this huge? Was he thinking of me—of a future—at all?

Nope, not going there.

I stick my head under the spray and recite a dozen go-to affirmations in my head about how strong and independent I am, about how I'll never let this man take advantage of me again.

Once I'm scrubbed from head to toe, I wrap a towel around my hair and giant bath sheet around my body. Then I stare at the door. He's on the other side, waiting. I know it. I feel it. And the longer I hide in here, the more he'll be convinced that I'm vulnerable to him. Afraid of him.

Fuck that.

Sucking in a fortifying breath, I open the bathroom door. A cloud of steam rushes out with me. And just as I thought, West is waiting about two inches from the portal, concern all over his face.

"Honey, talk to me."

"Nothing to say. A great orgasm on top of a long-ass day and a lot of stress lately... But don't worry." I wink. "You're great for relieving tension."

I breeze past him and head for my suitcase, praying my explanation will shut him up.

I should have known better.

He follows. "You connected with me."

"Well, you did have your penis inside my vagina, so...yep. We were definitely connected. Good observation."

As I bend to unzip my big suitcase, West grabs my wrist and tugs me upright. "That's not what I meant."

"If you're looking for something deeper than genital penetration, you're talking to the wrong girl."

West stares, watching me as I jerk free and paw through my clothes, looking for a nightgown and my toiletries. Finally, he cocks his head. "So this is how you're going to play tonight? We had a meaningless fuck and now it's over?"

Shit. He's gathering his thoughts, preparing an argument. If I don't stop this, he'll throw my stupid emotional outburst back in my face and use it as "evidence" to point out that I still have feelings for him.

"It doesn't have to be over..." I drop my towel.

His eyes go wide. His cock begins to swell and stand up.

Gotcha!

"In fact, I'm more than ready for round two, babe."

Before he can say another word, I take the situation— among other things—in hand, stroke his cock a few times, then sink to my knees. By the time I've wrapped my hands around his thighs and fastened my mouth on him, he's too far gone to do anything except let out a strangled gasp, thrust his fists in my hair, and start calling out for a higher power.

Over the next pleasurable while, I bring West to the brink of climax multiple times, then scale him back before release— all while doing my damnedest to ignore how his taste and musky scent affect me. Soon, he's growling and demanding and promising me all kinds of retribution. I ignore that and focus on precisely how to take him apart.

After all, he did the same to me.

I cup his balls, stroke my way up his shaft, run the edge of my teeth over the sensitive head, then suck him deep with a groan I know vibrates all the way down his length. Finally having power over him is heady.

Giving him an epic blow job arouses me, I admit. I'm human, and West is hot. But this is exactly how I want him—hard, gasping, wanting, and powerless to stop whatever I'm heaping on him.

He climaxes with a throaty shout, and I swallow him, laving and licking and savoring my triumph.

West staggers back to the bed. "Holy shit..."

I rise to my feet and give him a tight smile. "Like that?"

"You know I did." His eyes are nearly rolling back into his head from exhaustion. "Not the point..."

I glance at the clock on the nightstand. It's nearly eleven p.m. After two orgasms, I think I'm pretty safe putting the proverbial fork in him, so I'm all too happy to tuck him in.

"It seems like I filled the role of mistress pretty well this evening, Mr. Quaid. I hope you're pleased. But you have to be at work tomorrow, so I should let you get your rest."

"You sleep beside me," he manages to growl out.

But I hear exhaustion tugging at him. In another ten seconds, he'll be in dreamland.

"I'm right here." I lie beside him, doing my best to ignore the ache twinging again between my legs that I fear only he can put out. I'm stronger than it. Mind over matter. I will survive and all that. "Nighty night."

WEST

"You're packing up at"—my brother glances at his cell phone—"four fifteen? You never leave before seven, but you've run out of the office early every day this week like your ass was on fire. What's up?"

Leave it to Flynn to ask questions I'd rather not answer.

It's been five days since Eryn moved in as my mistress. Five days where I've spent every working hour wishing I was home with her. Four nights where she's managed to outwit and outmaneuver me for control. I'm determined that on this fifth night—even if it is a Friday the thirteenth—she will not blow-job her way out of letting me possess her body and penetrate the armor around her heart. Tonight, I've got to do better.

"Nothing," I lie casually.

"Really?" He raises a brow and shuts my office door, enclosing us in privacy—a must since we're both convinced Mom and Uncle Eddie have spies everywhere. "I thought it had something to do with the fact that you're with Eryn again."

I sigh in frustration. "Gen told you?"

"Of course. You know how she is."

"I really need to teach her the concept of keeping a secret."

Flynn's face softens. "She worries about you. We both do."

"It's not necessary. I'm a big boy."

"That doesn't mean you don't have feelings."

"Of course I do, but I've learned how to deal with them. Does anyone else know?"

"Neither of us has let anyone else in on the news."

"Thank you." Honestly, I don't think either would betray my confidence. Both of my siblings are on my side and would never use Eryn against me. They want me to be happy. I want the same for them.

"So...how are things going with your ex?" Flynn asks.

"Rocky."

"Eryn doesn't want to work it out so you can get back together?" When I shake my head, he scowls. "Then why is she with you? For the money?"

"No." I rush to calm his anger. "C'mon. You've met her. You know she's nothing like your ex."

"True. Besides, you're too smart to fall for a gold-digging snake in a tight dress. I was the idiot who let Tawny lead me around by my dick."

"Funny you should mention that particular problem..."

"Eryn is leading you around by yours?" Flynn raises a brow.

"Every damn night. I don't mean to let her, but the moment I get home, she's naked and waiting and she's so, so good on her knees..."

My brother laughs. "She found your Achilles' heel, huh? I get it. But if she's not after money, what does she want?"

"To fuck me out of her system. To get revenge for walking out on her."

He winces. "Ouch. Can you really blame her?"

"No, but I also can't let her get away again. She's the one. I just have to convince her of that." I sigh and sink into my chair. "First, I have to stop letting her attack my fly the minute I walk in the door and sucking out all my good intentions."

"That would help. Have a strategy?"

"Restrain her?"

Flynn seemingly considers the suggestion. "Would she go for that?"

Given the trust she doesn't have in me right now? "Probably not."

"Unless you want your reunion all over the tabloids, you shouldn't take her out. Mom would find out about Eryn in seconds."

And that would get ugly.

"That can't happen, not until I can manage the fallout."

As soon as I do, I will happily shock the family with my intentions.

"What are you going to do? Between her and Uncle Eddie—fucking climbers—they've got you by the balls. Unless you don't mind Mom finding some new and creative way to make Eryn's life unlivable."

"I mind *very* much." I rise, pace. Yes, I made Eryn attending a family dinner a condition of our contract, hoping more than believing that I could clear an easy path for her in my future. "I'm still thinking of a way to handle Mom. Do you know what Eddie is up to?"

"Besides peddling his usual song and dance about how he's the oldest living Quaid male so he should be running the show?"

"That's not going to fly with the board, and he should know that."

"You act like he's sober enough to process reality."

"You're right. My bad." My father's younger brother started partying in college and apparently never stopped. He even found a wife who loves to get sauced as much as he does. They're codependent enablers, and they will never change. "But since he's called for a vote of no confidence next week, he's clearly more determined than ever to seize the company."

Flynn nods. "I think he realizes he's getting older and you're doing a stellar job. If he doesn't talk the board into giving him a chance soon, he'll lose the opportunity forever."

"But, as far as you know, he doesn't have a specific plan?"

"Not that I can tell. He's schmoozing board members with linen-tablecloth lunches and expensive bottles of booze. I would hope most of them are smart enough not to fuck with their bottom line."

So if all remains status quo, the vote will go down this time just like the last. And that will take care of Eddie.

My mother is a completely different issue. She's determined to marry me off to a woman she chooses, one with the right pedigree who will be the perfect corporate wife, bolster my image, and make everyone in the family more money—especially her. No matter how many times I tell her that's not happening, she still persists, ever ready to blackmail me.

Miriam Quaid has never been a particularly warm human being. I don't know what my father ever saw in her. Since he died when I was in third grade, I can't exactly ask him. For years, I've wished she would remarry and start caring about something other than Quaid Enterprises. But she's proven again and again that she'll let no one come between her and her bank balance.

Flynn approaches and claps me on the back. "I'm heading out to New York this weekend. There's a...distraction I'd like to visit. While I'm there, I'll work on Mom. You concentrate on Eryn. And see if you can figure out what Eddie is up to, maybe pay the board members who might be wavering a visit to check their pulse. Have any ideas on how you'll handle the pair of vipers when the vote comes around?"

I nod. "Maybe it's time to get drastic where Mom is concerned. Being nice hasn't worked."

"It's never going to," Flynn seconded. "We sound so bent, plotting against the woman who gave birth to us."

"Those people don't know how self-serving she is." I rake a hand through my hair. "I miss Grandpa."

"I miss the old man, too. It doesn't seem like he's been gone three years..."

"As of next week, yes." I sigh.

Missing the old man and mourning him is something else that weighs on my mind, along with end-of-year financials, the upcoming board vote, my mom, my uncle...and Eryn. Always Eryn. I can't let her slip through my fingers.

"I'll let you get home." Flynn nods as he steps toward the closed door.

"Any advice?"

"To keep her from controlling you by your dick?" He shrugs. "I finally just had to cut Tawny out of my life altogether. I had a million reasons to, so it wasn't hard. You're in a different spot. My best advice is to stay one step ahead of her. You know that...but I'll bet the wrong head has been doing your thinking lately."

Yep. "Thanks. I'll give that some thought."

"Have a good weekend."

I wish him the same, then he's gone.

As my brain churns with ideas, I wave to my assistant, head out of the office, then hop in my Porsche. As I sit in a bitch of a traffic jam, I make a few phone calls until a great plan comes together.

It takes forty-five minutes to travel a few miles, but that's the Strip on a Friday evening. The bright side is, it's two minutes until six when I walk in the door.

Predictably, Eryn is waiting—naked except the cupless underwire bra necessary to support her lush tits. She's on her knees, looking at me with hunger in her bright eyes. "Welcome home."

When she reaches for my zipper, I grab her wrists and tug her to her feet. "It's good to be home. New rules for the weekend, honey. No more blow jobs."

She pales. "You love them."

"I do, and you know it way too well. But I haven't had a chance to feast on your body in days. Hell, I haven't even been inside you except your mouth. That changes tonight."

She jerks out of my grip. "But—"

"No buts. Did you bring a dress?"

"One. You said we'd be having dinner with your family."

"Eventually, I hope so. For now, put it on."

"But—"

I place a finger over her lips. "No more questions. Oh, and don't bother wearing panties beneath that dress. You're dessert."

Then I send a greedy smile in her direction and disappear into my bathroom. When I emerge from the shower and don fresh charcoal slacks and a white dress shirt, the door to Eryn's bathroom is closed. I frown. She spends a lot of time in there. In fact, most of the time—unless she's blowing me.

That's going to stop this weekend, too.

The sound of the penthouse's doorbell chimes through the place. I rush to the foyer and open the door to see a pair of waiters in white coats and tails rolling a cart off the elevator. "Good evening, Mr. Quaid. Where would you like dinner?"

I show them to the dining room. As I walk past the kitchen, it smells faintly like Eryn has been cooking. I rush to the stove and lift the lid off the pot. Some sort of chicken in a light wine sauce. I hope it will keep. Tonight I want her to enjoy what I've ordered just for her.

Ten minutes later, the fussy table I can't wait to get rid of is set to perfection. Candles are lit, the wine is resting, the silver-domed dishes look elegant next to the crystal glasses and crisp napkins. Behind me, I hear footsteps and whirl to get a look at Eryn.

I nearly swallow my tongue.

Her dress is red. Not a cheerful party red, like Christmas is just around the corner. But a blood red. A sexy red. The color of her flushed lips when I kiss them until they're swollen. The little sleeves rest off her shoulders and hug her arms. A crisscross of the satin clings to her breasts, then ends with the gather at her waist, encircling her where she's smallest. The skirt flares out gently and ends just above her knee. Matching lipstick, inky curls framing her face, and black peep-toe heels complete the ensemble.

"You look stunning," I manage to say.

She casts her gaze down for a moment, like she's not sure how to take my compliment, then looks up at me through the thick fringe of her lashes. She's not flirting, but the effect is a tease. My cock jerks in anticipation.

"Thanks," she murmurs. "You had dinner brought in. I cooked—"

"I saw. Will it keep until lunch tomorrow?"

She nods. "What did you order?"

I pull out her chair. "Sit down and you'll find out."

Eryn glances at me suspiciously as she complies. "You don't have to go to all this trouble. I'm here to serve you, remember? I pleasure you, feed you—"

"And derail me from having any sort of meaningful interaction with you." At her grimace, I sit beside her and take her hand. "Of course I figured it out. Did you think I wouldn't?"

"I'll be happy to try harder if my performance isn't good enough."

She's tossing the arrangement I dreamed up back in my face and trying to make me lose my temper. She's clever...but I'm not about to let her derail me.

"Honey, if your blow-job technique was any better, I'd be permanently wrung out and wearing a sated smile on my face twenty-four seven. You're intentionally missing the point. I want to be *with* you, not take pleasure *from* you."

She lifts one pale shoulder. "Semantics."

"Reality. Eat. Then we'll talk." I lift the lids off our domed plates and set them aside.

Savory aromas fill the air, along with her gasp.

"Lamb chops?" For the first time this evening, she looks softly surprised and rapt.

I don't bother repressing a smile. "Exactly the way you like them. Potatoes au gratin, roasted asparagus, a mixed green salad with feta, and sourdough rolls. All your favorites."

Her eyes actually fill with tears before she manages to blink them back. "You remembered."

"Whatever you think happened three years ago, I wanted to marry you because I loved you. I wanted to make you happy for the rest of your life." I lift her hand and press a kiss to her knuckles.

I want to tell her that nothing has changed. The words sit on the tip of my tongue, fighting to get past my lips. But I don't dare. She's not ready to hear them. In fact, I suspect they would have the opposite-than-intended effect. If I confess I'm still in love with her, her walls will rise between us. What little intimacy I've managed to wring from her will evaporate.

Instead, I watch, hoping like hell that she'll be curious enough, angry enough, or touched enough to ask me why. Why, if I loved her, did I leave her? Why, if I wanted to make her happy, did I disappear without an explanation?

But no. She presses her lips together and stares at the food, chin trembling.

"Eryn?"

She pastes on a plastic smile. "Everything looks amazing. Thank you."

I swallow back a curse. That's the most response I'm going to coax from her now. She had three years to learn to hate me and barely more than a week to accept that I'm back in her life.

"You're welcome." I grab a nearby remote and flip on some romantic R&B tunes, keeping the volume low. "What did you do today?"

"I went to the gym downstairs. I walked around the mall for a while. I watched a movie." She sighs. "I'm not used to having so little to do."

"A vacation isn't a bad thing."

She fidgets. "It's boring. Besides, if I was having a real vacation, I'd be with my sisters, doing something fun. Or trying to. Ella would suggest spa day. Echo would vote for mountain climbing. I'd play referee and cast the deciding vote, as usual."

I smile. I can totally picture that. I love that she's close with her sisters, despite the fact they're all vastly different women. "When was the last time you saw your parents? Did they go to Ella's wedding?"

"No. She got married last minute in North Carolina. Predictably, the folks just couldn't make it."

And there's her inner cynic, the one who believes no one really gives a shit about anyone but themselves, her sisters excepting.

"I haven't seen my mother in months," I venture, pouring us each a glass of wine.

She tilts her head as she slices into her lamb, then looks my way. "You never talked about your family much when... Well, before."

When we were engaged. She doesn't want to say the words. Because she doesn't want to be reminded? Because the memories hurt?

I shake my head. "I know. I didn't want to taint you. My mom isn't a happy person. She's always been difficult to be around, especially after Dad died. She grieved for a long while. Then she turned bitter, like life did her wrong. I've tried to understand. But..."

"I know. I do my best not to let my parents' indifference bother me too much, but when you're a kid and all the other mommies and daddies seem really involved and concerned while yours are working too much to give a shit? It's hard."

Eryn is clearly more comfortable discussing her workaholic parents' apathy than what went wrong between us. But at least we're skirting the topics that drove us apart. Maybe I can keep tiptoeing in this direction and steer the conversation back our way...

"It is. Your parents' behavior stunned me, I'll be honest."

She nods slowly. "At least they remembered to call Echo for her birthday in June."

But they obviously forgot Eryn's more recently.

"I'm sorry, honey. Really, really sorry." I take her hand again. "I think of you every September fifth."

"Thanks." She works her hand free and takes a bite of the lamb. "Hmm. That's *really* good."

I do the same, my head spinning with ways to broach the topic of our breakup. "Glad you like it."

She drags her fork through her potatoes and lifts a cheesy bite to her mouth. A second later, she's groaning. "Oh, these are incredible. I'm in love."

I laugh. "They're my favorite, too."

We eat and drink in silence for a few minutes. I let the

tension drain between us. I hold my impatience and try not to rush what might be the most important conversation we've had so far.

As she sets her fork down for the last time and wipes her mouth, I do the same. "Eryn, your parents' behavior isn't a reflection of you or anything you've done."

She nods. "I know that now."

But she didn't always, and it's one reason she's always been guarded. "They're human, and they have their own foibles and demons. My mom is the same."

"Did she ignore you growing up, too?"

"No. As an adult, she betrayed me. I don't speak to her except at public functions if the optics have to look good."

Eryn's face reflects confusion. "Betrayed you? In what way?"

I reach across the table and sandwich her hands between mine. "My mother is the reason we didn't get married three years ago, and I will never forgive her."

Eryn rips her hands free and leaps from her chair. "We didn't get married because you didn't want to."

She's halfway across the room, looking out the windows as night falls over the Strip and the city comes alive. Mentally, she's looking for an escape route again. I bite back a curse. I pushed too fast. It's frustrating, but I have to do everything at Eryn's pace. She's been preventing me from getting any closer to her this week, and I've been stupid enough to let her. Of course she doesn't want to hear that our broken engagement isn't my fault.

I approach her slowly. I know she's aware of me because

she stiffens. I stifle the urge to cup her shoulders, draw her closer. It would be a mistake.

"Eryn, you know my grandfather died nine days after I left you."

Her posture relaxes. She doesn't turn to face me, but I feel her sympathy. "Yes. I know you two were very close, and I'm sorry I never had the opportunity to meet him. He sounded like an incredible man."

"He was. I learned so much from him."

"My condolences. But he wasn't the only reason you left me on our wedding day."

"No. He also wasn't the only reason I couldn't come back to you right away and explain."

"You assumed the reins of Quaid Enterprises as soon as you got home?"

I nod. "I had to start fighting my uncle for the job. I swear, I wanted to call you a million times—"

"But you didn't, and now I'm just your temporary mistress." She turns to me and lifts her skirt up one thigh, baring her hip. "Where would you like your dessert, sir?"

Her question would turn me on if it wasn't delivered so emotionlessly. And it's telling that she'd rather risk exposing her emotions to me through a sexual interaction than a conversation.

"I owed you more than a phone call allowed," I argue.

"It's ancient history. Forget about it, West. I have."

That's the biggest lie she's ever told me, but I don't call her on it. Instead, I simply decide I've had enough.

On silent feet, I prowl toward her, closing the distance

between us, and tip her chin up with my finger until she's forced to meet my gaze. "I want my dessert in bed. Now."

CHAPTER SEVEN

ERYN

West is different tonight.

For the past few days, I managed to circumvent the unbearable intimacy he pushed on me by heaping pleasure on him first. That worked well, and he seemed content enough. Until now.

That look in his eyes tells me my strategy won't fly anymore.

Anxiety pops up. I shove it down. I'll be okay. I've had a few days to bolster my resistance to this man. It should be enough, right? It has to be because I can tell he intends to do his damnedest to surround my senses, penetrate my body, and steal my soul.

I raise my chin to escape his finger—and the resulting burn from that one simple touch. I look away to find my composure, which I nearly lost after one hungry stare. My heart thuds so hard it's nearly painful. My breaths score my lungs. Every sense is attuned to Weston Quaid and the resolution on his face. Yeah, there will be no eluding him with a simple blow job tonight.

"Would you like me clothed or naked?" I'm proud of how calm I sound.

"Don't do this, Eryn."

"What?"

"Talk to me dispassionately, like you're a fucking waitress asking if I want coffee or tea."

"I *am* a waitress."

"Right now you're my mistress."

"And that's all I'll ever be. Maybe you've forgotten, Mr. Quaid, that nothing in our contract says I have to feel anything for you, simply be present. So here I am, living up to my end of the bargain. Clothed or naked?"

West's jaw clenches. I'm pushing his temper. He wants me to shelve my resistance and embrace him again as if he didn't completely tear my world apart three years ago.

Finally, his expression flattens. He's reached some decision. I have a bad feeling about this...

"Turn around." He makes the accompanying motion with his finger.

Swallowing and hoping he can't see my nerves, I comply. But I'm worried... West will be methodical in searching for any weaknesses he can exploit. I have to hope that he finds orgasm before I come apart.

One warm hand cups my nape. The other pulls at the tab of my zipper. As he tugs it down, a sensual hiss fills the air. I suck in a breath as he shoves the sleeves down my arms. The dress slithers to the floor. With a flick of his fingers, he makes quick work of my strapless bra.

Then I'm standing before him, trembling and utterly exposed. I feel his stare all over my ass.

I glance over my shoulder at him as he holds out his hand.

Automatically, I lay my fingers on his upturned palm.

"Step out."

As I do, tingles crackle down my spine. Already, the ache between my legs is sharp and lip-bitingly strong.

To my surprise, he retrieves the dress from the floor, then lays it over the nearest chair. The bra he tosses on the seat, then he glides a palm possessively down my waist, over my hip, then cups my derrière. "Walk."

"I'm leaving the shoes on?"

"For now."

There's nothing left to say, so I head for his bedroom, trying to ignore my nerves and my heart lodged in my throat.

When I cross the threshold, I turn to him. "On the bed?"

"Yes. Legs spread."

What does he want? What is he planning? I don't know, and the suspense is killing me. I could ask...but then he'd know the answer mattered to me. Besides, in this mood, I'm not convinced he'd divulge anything. I don't know precisely what he's seeking from me. I know what he *says* he wants. Me. Us together. But I've heard this before. Maybe he even believes he means it this time. But if I give in, he'd probably sing the same song, different verse, before he disappears. Then I'd be alone again.

No.

With a nod, I dip my knee onto the mattress and climb to the middle, then flip over to brace myself on my elbows, acutely aware of his stare. Slowly, I part my thighs, high heels gliding across the stiff brocade duvet.

"Stop."

Instantly, I cease everything but my breathing. That's one thing I can't control. In the silent room, it's choppy and audible.

His stare rakes my exposed breasts, dip of my stomach, my thighs...and everything in between. If a gaze can be a tactile caress, I feel his. The tingle of it charges through me, electric and undeniable.

"You're wet."

Why deny what he can visibly see? "Yes."

"You're aroused."

"Yes."

"Touch yourself."

I freeze. "Where?"

But I know the answer.

"Drag your fingers through that pussy. Give your clit a tease." He walks closer as he watches me dip my fingers into my sex and skim my nerve-laden button with a back-arching hiss. "Stop. Show me your fingers."

I hesitate, desperate to give myself relief. If I do, maybe I won't ache so much for him. And maybe I'm fooling myself since the ache is way worse now that I know he's here and watching.

I don't know what game West is playing with me or why I'm responding so utterly. My desire is so intense, it's scary. The lack of control I have over my body while he's toying with me is even more terrifying.

Suddenly, he grabs my wrist and drags my hand away from my sex. "I said stop."

At the feel of his fingers clamping around my arm, my

breathing roughens. The tension between us climbs. My ache deepens.

He turns his attention to my fingers, smiling with sly pleasure. "Drenched."

I don't answer; there's nothing to say. Then it doesn't matter because he sucks my fingers into the warm cavern of his mouth with a moan and steals my breath.

After he licks me thoroughly, the tip of his tongue tracing the seam between my digits, he releases me to trail kisses down my palm and up the sensitive skin of my inner arm. Climbing onto the bed, he hovers over me, lips drifting toward the crook of my elbow. Once there, he nips at the delicate flesh, making my breath catch, before he licks his way up my biceps, sucks at my collarbone, then nuzzles my neck.

Every move is pure seduction, and I don't know how to resist. I want to be angry with him. Actually, I want to feel nothing for him, but every emotion is converging like a twister in my heart. Resentment, mistrust, hurt—all still there. But less welcome feelings are creeping in, like empathy.

I had no idea the relationship between him and his mother was so strained. My curiosity surges. What happened? What could she possibly have done to prevent West and me from marrying?

But it's the unavoidable chemistry he and I share that gets to me every time. Sexual, yes. But in the reckless moments where I forget our past, I find myself liking him. Enjoying the time I spend with him. I even let myself be touched that he remembers my favorite foods. To most people, it would seem simple and silly. But, other than my sisters, he's the only person who's ever cared.

Does it mean something I'm too afraid to hear?

"Eryn?"

I blink, back in the moment. "What?"

"Spread your legs wider."

I do, trying to resist a fresh twinge of excitement. But it's futile. Four words—that's all he has to utter—before I'm trembling to comply.

"Like that." He nods as he maneuvers his wide shoulders between them and pins me with a greedy, hot stare. "Perfect."

A wave of heat rolls through me. I close my eyes. If I don't look at him, maybe I won't feel as attuned to him?

He chuckles as if he can read my mind. "Open your pussy for me."

The command hits me with another blast of heat. I know exactly what he's doing. With one sentence, West is forcing me helplessly onto my back and insisting I expose every bit of my most intimate self to him for his consumption.

But am I upset? Is my first urge to call him a bastard and tell him to piss off? No, my body is a traitor, and even while my head is screaming, I follow his dictate.

"Hmm." He glides a finger down the soft, bare pad of my sex. "I've dreamed of this all day. All week. But there's nothing to interrupt us now, and I know exactly where I want to spend my weekend."

His words alone make me clench. Then he slides one thick finger into my empty, clutching opening. My body seizes on him greedily. But he doesn't move to give me relief, simply enjoys watching my arousal climb.

The fact that he has more control over my body than I do is both horrifying and hot as hell.

I'm still trying to process that reality when his shoulders butt against the back of my thighs and the crook of my knees fall into his grip. His exhalations singe my sex. I shudder.

"Open your eyes. Look at me."

If I do, I'll unravel. "You don't need me to do that for what you have in mind."

"But I want you to. I'm going to have more of you than merely your orgasms."

He wants my soul.

Fear shoots through my heart. Desire twists my stomach.

All those days I spent fortifying my defenses against him? Pointless. I'm already open to him in almost every way; he's seen to that. And since Weston Quaid has me right where he wants me, I don't see how I'll stop him from taking all of me.

Slowly, I lift my lashes. "Don't do this."

He rakes a tongue through my furrow, lingering at my clit. Tingles burn and spread. My whole body tightens. I arch, gasp.

"Will you hate me for loving you?" he asks.

I don't think I can. And for that, it's myself I hate.

He glides a palm up my thigh and plants kisses along the tender skin. "Give me the weekend to show you this time will be different."

I don't reply. First, because he doesn't wait for me to. He simply lowers his head and gives his mouth full reign over my body. Every nook, cranny, and sensitive spot he thinks needs attention, he claims and conquers. His lips cover my folds. His tongue makes love to my clit. And I'm helpless against him.

The first orgasm takes me like a slow-gathering storm, brewing and swirling, building, building...then releasing with a sudden slam of pleasure that leaves me stunned, shaken, and breathless. The second is all stealth, a thief in the night, waiting, stalking, finding my weakest moment to steal over me and rob me of thoughts and common sense. The third is the most catastrophic, a giant behemoth that seizes on the lingering ache from my previous climaxes and manipulates for long, aching minutes, uncaring how much I twist or beg for relief. It sits like a gleeful soul-stealing demon, a breath from granting me deliverance. Only when I claw and give him a teary promise to surrender all of me does he allow me to crest the pinnacle that strips my throat raw from screaming and sends my heart slamming uncontrollably against my chest.

Then it's over. Blinking, I realize the magnitude of what I've ceded to West. Worse, I can't take it back.

Seemingly gratified that he's taking me apart, he calmly watches my chest heave and my body shudder while he dons a condom. "You're flushed and beautiful."

No, I'm destroyed.

Then he kneels between my sprawled legs and gathers my thighs in his palms, settling himself in between. He laves his way up the side of my breast before lying on top of me. Our chests press together. Our faces are so close, I can smell my musk on his skin.

"West..." His name is a plea for mercy. If he keeps at this, he's going to turn me inside out. I'm going to free-fall back into something dangerously close to love.

His smile says he knows it. And that he won't give me an ounce of mercy.

MISADVENTURES WITH MY EX

"You look like this in all my fantasies, you know." West slides a hand between us to fit the head of his cock against my slick opening and nudges gently, letting me feel exactly how swollen I am. "Lovely. Yielding." A grin plays at his lips before he plants his palms on the mattress and surges inside me with all his strength. "Mine."

He fills up every inch of me, his cock burning a path through my body seemingly made for him. Ten seconds ago, I would have sworn I barely had the energy to move. But he's like a lightning rod inside me, jolting every sated muscle back to screaming life.

I don't even think before I throw my arms around him and plant my mouth over his.

With a groan, he sinks deep there, too, sliding his tongue along mine, filling me in every way he can.

Arousal seeps back under my skin, pooling between my legs, greedy and growing with each and every one of his slow, rough thrusts.

"You've always been mine," he insists as he burrows impossibly deeper.

I shake my head. But I can't push a "no" past my lips when he's claiming my mouth again.

He tears his lips free. "Yes. You'll always be mine."

"For thirty-seven days."

"Don't fool yourself."

Then the talking stops and the seduction starts again. West is not only perceptive but relentless, seeming to know exactly where to touch me and when, what to whisper in my ear, how to use every touch to further weaken my defenses. I'm breathless, clinging and sobbing, as the pleasure licking flames under my skin converge into a blaze where we're joined. With long, strong, systematic strokes, he undoes me a little more with each moment.

Suddenly, the peak I was sure I was too sated to have before he tunneled inside me becomes the most devastating orgasm of the night. Maybe of my life. Black spots dance in my vision as I howl out in sweating, grinding, unceasing pleasure. My only anchor in the world is West, rocking above me as he juts and jolts through his own crest, shouting my name.

Wilting against the damp sheets, I try to dredge up the energy to get away to the bathroom and put distance between us. I have to. The ecstasy proved utterly destructive to my protective walls. I feel myself wide open and bleeding out for West.

I close my eyes, but tears still leak from the corners. If I don't get some time and space away from him, I'm going to break down and admit that I've missed him, that I need him. That I don't think I ever fell out of love with him.

Above me, he shifts. I hear the nightstand drawer opening and frown. Is he ready for another round and reaching for a fresh condom? Does he think I'm not already in a puddle at his feet?

Then I feel him tug my wrist just before something constricts around it, holding it in place.

I open my eyes and glance up my arm in disbelief. The son of a bitch tied me to the bed.

"What the hell are you doing?"

"Preventing you from escaping to the shower. On Sunday,

I stupidly gave you the opportunity to hide in the bathroom. I'm not letting it happen again. Now you can't run while we should be talking."

Is he kidding?

That resolution is back on his face. He's not kidding at all.

"I don't want to talk."

My response is childish; I'm aware of that. But now that he's stripped me so bare, I'm afraid that whatever he has to say will change everything and I'll be forced to decide whether to trust him again. I'm not ready. I don't know if I'll ever be.

He clenches his teeth. "Then you can listen. I didn't leave you because I didn't love you. Or didn't want to marry you. Despite what you think, I always intended to slide that wedding band on your finger. The morning of the wedding, my mother called."

"And told you that you couldn't marry me or you'd be disinherited. I get it." That shouldn't hurt anymore, but it does.

"No. That was her first threat. I told her I didn't care. First, she didn't have the power to make that happen. Second, I'm smart. I can make my own money." West heaves a frustrated sigh. "Back then, you kept asking me why only Flynn and Genevieve were attending our wedding from my side of the family. I'm going to tell you."

"It doesn't matter. It's ancient history."

"That's still haunting us today. Remember how we met?"

"At that crappy bar where I used to work. So?"

For the first time, he hesitates, like he's finally reluctant to open a can of worms. "My grandfather sent me to meet you. To romance you."

My thoughts race, and I can't think of a single reason I would have been on Hanover Quaid's radar. "Why?"

"Your dad started working on a story for the network to air on the evening news. It was an exposé about building superintendence and maintenance practices in Southern California that supposedly put workers and apartment dwellers at risk. We'd just started property management in that market, and he was looking hard at us because we were struggling to comply with the seismic building codes that seemed to change day by day, city by city. We knew we'd get there, but my grandpa was convinced that if you and I were an item, your dad might back off the story long enough for us to catch up."

Betrayal I swore I wasn't capable of feeling for this man anymore stabs me in the heart. "So none of what we had was even real?"

"It was real, honey." He winces. "But at the start, I wasn't honest or ethical. I'm sorry for that. But I can't regret anything because it led me to you."

Bullshit wrapped in pretty words. "Your scheme worked. My dad backed off the story shortly before we married. And once he did, you called the wedding off."

"No. That's not what happened. There's more. A lot more. About two weeks after we hooked up, I called my grandfather and told him you were everything I wanted. Independent. Gutsy. Prickly. But somehow funny and warm and interesting. I admitted that I was falling for you." He cups my face as if willing me to believe him. "Eryn, I had never met a woman like you, and that's saying something since my mother paraded a few hundred in front of me whom she thought had the pedigree to marry the next Quaid heir. I hated them all. They were *so* into appearances. Vain. Vapid. Self-absorbed. You weren't just new and shiny. You were genuine. You would never marry for money. Or prestige. Hell, you barely knew who I was."

"When we first met? Only vaguely."

"Exactly." He nods enthusiastically, as if he's glad I'm seeing this his way. "Once I told my grandfather how I felt about you, he was totally in favor of us. Whoever made me happy, that's who he wanted me to marry, so I had his full support when I told him I intended to propose. While you and I were planning the wedding, he learned he had colon cancer and that he'd let it go too long. Within weeks, his health started to falter."

"When you told me that he was terminal, I asked you if you needed to go home and be with your family. You said no."

"Because my grandfather pointed out that it didn't change his prognosis. He loved me and I loved him. We knew it. We both agreed you were more important. So I stayed. But my mother started putting pressure on me to come home to assume the reins of Quaid Enterprises before my worthless uncle, her rival, did. In the last conversation I ever had with my grandpa, he made me promise to stay in LA and marry you. He swore he'd make it long enough for me to make you my wife and have a week's honeymoon."

West's face twists as he fights tears. Despite my resentment and confusion, I can't stop myself from reaching out to comfort him. "West, don't say anything else. The explanation doesn't matter anymore."

"I need to keep going. I owe you this." He frowns and sucks in a breath, gathering his determination. "My grandfather did his best to keep his side of the bargain. He used all his grit to last nine days after what would have been our wedding. He was the toughest man I ever knew."

Despite how furious I am, my heart hurts for him. His grief is so palpable that it moves me. I stroke his arm, cup his shoulder, silently giving him my strength. West looks as if he needs it badly.

"Thanks." He squeezes me in return. "Like I said, the problem was my mother."

"You said that before. I don't understand."

"It's simple. She wanted me to marry someone who would look good on my arm, who would ensure the board chose me over my uncle when the vote to replace my grandfather went down. She was looking for a pretty, well-bred bride to 'guide.' Her philosophy was if she could control my wife and my wife could pussy-whip me..."

"Then she could control you, too."

"Precisely. She never planned on you. On the morning of our wedding, she discovered I intended to marry you. She went nuclear."

"How did she find out?" He'd been so careful to keep everything a secret, and until now I never knew why.

"Social media. Echo posted that she was excited it was our wedding day. She tagged me. My mother saw."

"So if she didn't threaten to disinherit you, what did she say?"

"She threatened to confront you, spill the fact that you and I met under false pretenses. She intended to convince you that I was scamming you. Somehow, she had obtained the emails my grandfather and I exchanged, plotting the best way for me to meet you, stressing that I needed to accelerate our relationship so I could get to your father fast. And if that alone didn't persuade you to end our engagement, Mom had a whole spiel planned to 'prove' that I intended to leave you at the altar. Since you'd always found trust difficult, I worried..." He rakes a hand through his hair. "That you would believe her. And you would leave me."

Back then? I want to say he was wrong and that I wouldn't have listened to his mother for a minute. That I loved him too much for that. But I don't know. Even then, I thought West was almost too good to be true. When he walked away from me, it seemed to prove all my instincts right.

"As soon as I hung up on my mother, I planned to drive over to your place and confess everything before the ceremony. But my grandfather collapsed. They rushed him to the hospital. That's when I called to tell you that I had to leave and hopped on a plane. Grandpa spent his remaining days in a coma, and I spent them trying to keep my uncle from seizing control of the company while grieving the imminent loss of the man who'd always been my father figure and worrying I'd lose you forever. I always intended to come back and marry you. Always," he growls with conviction. "During my grandfather's funeral, she let me know that if I even called you—much less married you—before the board voted me in as CEO, she would make your life absolute hell. And she can do it. By the time I had full control of the business, so much time had passed. You had moved, changed your number, switched jobs." He stares at me, letting me see his stark pain. "You were gone."

When I realized West wasn't coming back, I did my best to remove every reminder of him from my life. "Why did your grandfather target me in the first place? Why not Ella or Echo?"

"Math. Ella was older and less likely to take an undergrad seriously. Echo was underage. That left you." West takes my hands. "And I'm grateful. Yeah, what my grandfather and I planned wasn't right, but I knew Quaid Enterprises wasn't doing anything wrong...just learning a new market. We couldn't let your dad's segment about us air, or it would be a financial disaster for the company. We knew we'd eventually be vindicated, but with only a few months in LA under our belts, we couldn't take a chance. Since I was attending UCLA and you were working around the corner...I didn't see the harm in flirting with you. But I also didn't expect to fall like a ton of bricks. So things got sticky. I wanted to tell you everything. I'd always planned to after we were married. I'd hoped by then it wouldn't matter because you'd know I loved *you*."

Right now, I don't know anything except that I have to think all this through. "I need some time to myself, West."

He shakes his head. "We're finally getting to the truth. If I leave you alone, all you'll do is build up more walls between us. I've come too far to lose you again. I still love you, and I am not giving up on us this time. In fact, I'm never giving up on us again."

His speech is so heartfelt, it's hard not to believe him. On the other hand, he was the man I thought I was going to spend my life with and he utterly broke my heart. How do I get past that?

"If all of this is true, you've had this knowledge for three years. I've had it for less than fifteen minutes. I need to wrap my head around it. Alone. Just one night. Please."

WEST

The last thing in the world I want to do is leave world-weary Eryn alone with her thoughts for a whole night. But after the ways I fucked up then barged back into her life...if that's what she wants, how can I refuse her?

For what seems like the hundredth time, I toss and turn on the sofa, try to reshape my pillow to find some semblance of comfort. Nothing. Sure, I would have been more comfortable in one of the spare bedrooms, but I couldn't be that far from the door in case Eryn decided during the night to leave me for good. Not that she wouldn't be justified.

Looking back, I see a hundred ways I should have handled things differently...like been more honest with Eryn once I realized I was in love with her. I should have believed more in the strength of our love. I should have lived up to the promise I made Grandpa and stayed in LA to marry Eryn. But I was twenty-one and overwhelmed by how quickly my life was unraveling. If I had a do-over... But I don't. I can only deal with my reality now.

And I've made a goddamn mess.

I glance at my phone. It's four a.m. in Vegas, which means it's after seven in New York. Flynn is back there keeping tabs on Mom this weekend. Maybe he's awake. If not...it won't be the first time one of us has woken the other up for a crisis.

On the fourth ring, my brother answers with a groggy "'lo."

"Can you talk?"

I hear sheets rustling as he fumbles upright. "West?"

"Yeah. If I'm interrupting something..."

"She's asleep. Let me find someplace private..." He stands, and I hear his footsteps on the creaky floors.

"So it's going well with your 'distraction'?"

I hear a door shut. "She's a way to pass time—albeit one with a really banging body—but nothing permanent." He sounds surprisingly bummed by that fact. "By the way, thank you for moving Quaid Enterprises to Vegas once you took over."

"With West Coast operations booming, I didn't really have a choice."

"True, but I'd forgotten how freaking cold it gets back here. I'll take the summer heat in Nevada any day over this shitty-ass winter. I was downtown last night, cutting through the courtyard of the 9/11 Museum to get from Greenwich to West. The reflection pools are sobering enough, but the stiff wind cut through my coat and I had to get naked to get warm, if you know what I'm saying."

Despite everything, I chuckle. "Pansy."

"Hey, I like sun. Sue me," Flynn grouses. "Okay, I'm in her kitchen, searching for the coffee. What's up?"

I take a deep breath. "I told Eryn everything."

"And what was her reaction?"

"I'm not sure. She wanted to be alone tonight."

Flynn doesn't say anything for a long time. "Can you blame her?"

"No. But I have to do better this time. I have to figure out some way to prove to her that we're strong enough to get past this, that I'll be here for her, that—"

"She has to forgive you first."

"And I don't know if she ever will."

"Given the way things went down, she must feel like everything and everyone else was more important to you than her."

And that I utterly let her down. "Yeah."

"You want her back?"

"Absolutely. I want to marry her." The more time I spend with Eryn, the more I know I'm meant to be with her.

"Then you gotta make her feel special, bro. You've got to find some way to prove that she comes first and that you'll never let anyone else come between you two again."

Easier said than done, especially since I need an epic way to convince her. "I also have to get past this board meeting next Friday, squash Eddie's claims once and for all, then tell Mom she can either accept the woman I want to marry or get out of my life."

"Watch yourself. She won't take that lying down."

"I'm prepared for that."

"Are you? Really? Think of the most devious thing she could do to undermine you. Then multiply it by a hundred. I'm not sure your creativity stretches that far."

I'm not sure anyone's does. "I've got some ideas. Is Mom still planning to winter in Vegas?"

"Yep. I verified that when I had dinner with her last night. She'll be flying in on Tuesday. But she knows something is up. She's got eyes and ears everywhere. She's well aware you haven't kept your usual hours at the office this week. She also knows you haven't been out partying and hooking up. She's determined to find out what you're doing."

My guts seize. So I have three days—maybe four—to repair my relationship with Eryn and figure out how I'll prevent my mother and her greed from coming between us again. "Thanks for the warning."

"You're welcome. I'll be flying back with her. I'll keep her occupied as long as I can, but you know how she can be…"

Do I ever. "Thanks. I owe you."

"I'll remember that if I ever find a woman I love enough to fight for."

We end the call, and I'm alone with my thoughts. I stand, pace. Think. Plot. Ideas spin and fill my head while I sip coffee. I have Eryn completely to myself without any distractions this weekend. But by the time the cup is empty, I still have no great ideas on how to win her back. The sex has been beyond, but she needs more than pleasure from me. She needs to feel cherished and beloved.

She needs me to put her first. I've got to do that—starting now.

Tiptoeing across the penthouse, I slowly open my bedroom door. Thankfully, it's silent, and I ease toward the bed to check on Eryn, curled into a ball on her side of the bed.

To my surprise, she rolls over. "What are you doing?"

"Checking on you. Why aren't you asleep?"

"I haven't slept all night." Her voice sounds scratchy and a little nasally. She's been crying.

That hurts. "I haven't either. I know you wanted tonight to yourself, but maybe we'll do better working our issues out together."

She shakes her head, her dark, silky hair brushing her shoulders. "I can't think around you. You overwhelm me. You always have. When you're in my personal space, it's like all I can see are the sun and rainbows and good things. I never see what's actually lurking under all that pretty stuff until it bites me."

I risk coming closer and sit on the edge of the bed to take her hand in mine. "There's nothing lurking underneath this time. I'm sorry I didn't tell you the truth. I wanted to protect you from the ugly family politics. I still do."

"They don't matter anymore. We're just temporary."

There's a note of hurt in her whisper that spurs me to take her in my arms. She's stubbornly refusing to believe I'll never let her go again. Because when I waltzed back into her life, I strong-armed her into becoming my mistress, rather than groveling, apologizing, and trying to make her my fiancée again?

I can fix that.

"How about we get out of here?" I suggest.

In the shadows, I see her surprise. "And go where? You must be exhausted, too."

Actually, now that I have some direction, I'm exhilarated. "Nope. Pack for an overnight stay. I've got a surprise."

CHAPTER EIGHT

ERYN

Thirty minutes later, West tosses our luggage into his sleek black Porsche. We hop inside and jet down I-15 in the dark. I have no idea where he's taking me. He simply turns the heater on, flips on the satellite radio to something soothing, then tells me to lie back and relax.

When I wake again and sit up, the sun is shining and we're on I-10 approaching downtown LA.

I blink. "Where are we going?"

"I'm taking you home."

For good? My heart lurches in my chest. Now that he got his past off his chest and figured out he can still unravel me anytime he wants, he's letting me go?

Pain seizes me... I didn't expect to feel it—or anything—for him ever again. I thought I knew better. I'd hoped I managed to protect myself. But why lie? I've suspected for almost a week that he was getting to me. Now it's undeniable that I'm falling hard and fast for Weston Quaid once more.

And he's walking away.

What's wrong with me? What flaw do I have that leaves me mooning and weeping over a man who always says the right things, makes love to me like I'm the only woman he'll ever care for, then discards me once he's through?

"Fine." I lean as far away from him as his sporty ride allows. "You can send me the rest of my things when you get back to Vegas."

He sighs heavily and grabs my hand. Even though I stiffen against his pull, he lifts my palm to his lips. "Honey, I'm not dropping you off. And I'm certainly not leaving you. Haven't you been listening to me at all?"

I don't answer. He knows what I'm thinking. I heard him, but...

"You don't believe me yet. Seriously, I'm never leaving you. If you want to be rid of me, you'll have to be the one to go."

I cut a glance in his direction. He seems serious. I want to believe him.

Hope, the insidious bastard, takes root in my heart. My brain is telling me to take a wait-and-see approach. I should listen to the smarter of my two organs.

Finally, we pull up at my apartment complex. West collects our luggage and escorts me upstairs. When I let us in, familiar surroundings greet me. They should soothe me. But after a week in West's palatial, Vegas-ostentatious pad, my simple unit full of artfully cultivated garage-sale and clearance-bin finds doesn't feel like home anymore.

He leads me to the bedroom and drops our suitcases near my closet, then starts peeling away my sweatshirt and athletic pants.

"What are you doing?" I push at his hands. I don't know where I stand with him, and I don't understand why we're in

LA. Sex isn't going to help any of that.

West sighs. "Letting you sleep. That's why I brought you to your place."

I scowl in confusion. "Just for sleep?"

"You didn't get any last night. I thought you'd rest better in your own bed."

My jaw drops. Is he for real? He drove three hundred miles simply so I could be more comfortable? Regardless of the fact that he hasn't slept and would have felt more chill in his own penthouse?

"I don't understand what's happening between us," I finally murmur.

He gathers me close. I don't resist...but I don't melt against him, either.

"The last week has been a lot for us both to digest. I've changed your whole routine, uprooted you, made you start thinking about a future you thought was dead. You've made me realize what a colossal mistake it was not to fight harder for us three years ago. You're full of confusion. I've got regrets." He squeezes me tighter. "But we can get through this together."

I don't know what to say. I don't know whether he's right or whether we're both crazy. One thing, though. We want the same conclusion. We both want us, together. I wish I could deny it. I tried to. It didn't work. I don't know how I'll trust West again, but I already know that stubbornly insisting there's nothing left between us but sex is pointless.

"Maybe."

"That's better than you telling me to fuck off," he quips. "I'll take it for now. C'mon. Lie down. Rest."

The stubborn part of me wants to sit up and talk. Exhaustion has other plans. When he strips away the rest of my clothes, then peels off his own and pulls me down to my cool white sheets and into his arms, I can't keep my eyes open.

But when I wake, he's gone.

I sit up, feeling West's absence immediately. A glance around tells me it's early afternoon. His suitcase is missing.

Son of a bitch.

Then I hear the front door shut.

"West?"

"Yeah. You awake, honey?"

He came back?

He said he wasn't leaving. Maybe this time you should believe him...

"Where did you go?"

"To run a few errands before I take you somewhere special tonight. And to grab some lunch. You have no food in this house that isn't frozen." He appears in the door of the bedroom, looking put out by my extensive Lean Cuisine selection.

I wince. "Sorry. Since I'm only here long enough to scarf down a few calories before I crash for the night, things like grocery shopping don't always happen."

He holds up a bag from a local sandwich shop I love. "Well, here I am, coming to your rescue."

Climbing from the bed, I stretch and yawn—catching sight of his duffel in my bathroom. He must have taken a shower while I snoozed. "My hero."

West drops the subs on my dresser and prowls toward me, his stare raking my naked body. "Yes, ma'am. How hungry are you for that turkey on wheat?"

"Starved."

"Are you sure?" He nuzzles my neck and palms my waist. "There's no way for me to talk you into waiting, oh, an hour to eat?"

Managing to hold in my shiver, I give him a little shove. "I know you. An hour will become two. Then I'll waste away."

The truth is, if I give in to him while I'm feeling so confused and vulnerable, my head will be too cloudy to hear anything he says. We need to talk way more than we need to fall into bed together.

At least that's what I'm telling my eager body.

He sighs and scoops up the sandwiches. "Fine. I'll grab bottles of water and set up in the kitchen."

"Thanks," I call after him.

After digging my robe out of the closet, I head out to the main living space of my unit and find him spreading our food and a couple of bags of chips across my bistro table.

"Feel better?" West takes a bite and moans like he's savoring it. "Damn. Apparently, I was hungry, too."

Since we skipped breakfast, that doesn't surprise me.

"We both needed the sleep." And I needed time to get a fresh perspective. "You got some, right?"

"A few hours. It's enough."

I scarf down half my sandwich in the same time it takes him to devour all of his. In between bites, I regard him across the table. "I can't believe you drove all the way here just to let me sleep in my own bed."

West tosses his napkin aside, then reaches for my hands.

"When we were together before, I didn't put you first when you needed me to the most. I'm going to do that from now on. And I know your cynical heart. You either don't believe me yet or you're not sure what to think. That's what this weekend is for, so I can prove to you how serious I am."

"What do you want, West?"

"You."

"Beyond the next thirty-six days?"

"Yes. Screw our arrangement. I don't want a mistress. I just didn't know how else to persuade you to come to Vegas and spend time with me so we could see what was left of us."

I nod slowly. As much as I hate to admit it, I understand his point. "All right. Then I...have questions."

"I'm sure you do. Fire away."

"Did you ever feel guilty for romancing me under false pretenses?"

He pauses. "At first, yeah. When I took you to bed the night we met, I felt like I had an angel on one shoulder telling me this was wrong, that you could get hurt...and a devil on the other insisting we'd enjoy the hell out of each other. And since you said you weren't looking for anything lasting, what harm could I really be doing? As long as I treated you well while we were together and found an amicable way to make your dad back away from the story, how could anything go wrong? Before long, I started falling for you." He sighed. "I talked to my grandfather a few times about coming clean, but we both agreed it would be best to wait until after you and I were married. Then you'd know I genuinely loved you. After all, if I was only with you to make your dad back off, he already had.

Why go through with the wedding?"

"But then you didn't."

"And now you know why. I also suspected that if I confessed everything then, you'd never believe or forgive me. And I was torn up about my grandfather while so damn worried we'd never be together again. I...froze. I wish I'd handled everything differently. Time and maturity have taught me a lot. But I can't go back. So here we are now."

"Who was the woman you took to the theater the week after you left me?"

West scans his memory, then rolls his eyes. "Someone my mother foisted off on me. For the record, I never touched her."

"But you weren't celibate for three years."

"No. Once I realized I'd truly lost you, I tried to move on. I failed pretty miserably. I guess you didn't do a lot better?"

How much do I confess? If he's being honest and we're really working on bridging the chasm between us, shouldn't I tell him everything? "I...slept with one of your frat brothers about two weeks after your grandfather's funeral." When he rears back like I've slapped him, I rush to explain. "By then, I thought all your family stuff must be over. But you hadn't called. You hadn't returned any of my calls, either. And I saw you on TMZ with that woman..."

"I don't remember her name. I never even saw her again. I certainly didn't fuck her. I was working fourteen-hour days, six days a week, at a multibillion-dollar organization I barely understood, while trying to finish up school and keeping my mother off your back. I missed you like hell." He clenches his teeth. "So, your revenge...was it sweet?"

"No." I tear up because as much as I've blamed West for everything, I have some guilt in all this, too. "I regretted having sex with that douche immediately. I told him never to call me again."

He looks away, his face twisting with sadness. "You had every right to be angry."

"But not to intentionally sleep with someone you knew simply to stab you in the back. It was low. I felt awful."

West sighs and takes my hands. "Look, neither of us have been completely alone while we've been apart. It's water under the bridge now. I just want to move forward."

It should be, but even knowing he's given another woman the kind of attention and pleasure he gives me makes me crazy. "Is it?"

"Whatever you did while we were apart, I don't love it. And I can't blame you...but I don't want to hear more."

I drag in a breath. He's right, and I shouldn't let the past continue to be a stumbling block between us. "All right. Same."

"Anything else?"

"Yeah." She frowns. "If you don't get along with your uncle, and your mom is going to try to shred me, why did you insist in our agreement that I attend a family dinner?"

"When I put that into our negotiations, I hoped that you and I would decide to try getting back together. Mom will be an obstacle until we show her that nothing she says or does can tear us apart again. I always intended to prepare you beforehand so you wouldn't be blindsided by her venom. But I have to be honest, she's not going to take this lying down. Expect something."

"Sounds like it will be an uncomfortable dinner, but I can handle her."

"My uncle will probably just be a leering drunk."

"I've endured plenty of those waiting tables over the years."

"I have no issue putting him in his place so you don't have to."

"Okay."

"You'll do it?"

What West is really asking me is if I'm willing to brave his family because I'm committed to trying to make things work between us again. I hesitate. It's not that I'm unsure; there's really no other option except to see where we could take our relationship. If I don't, I'll always wonder *what if*. But this is a big step. West seems to be all in. I was last time...and I got burned. I'm still a little scared. Okay, a lot. No, having my heart broken again isn't the worst thing that could happen, but it isn't an experience at the top of my list to repeat. Still, was I actually happier alone?

"Dinner it is."

The smile that brightens his face is wide and elicits thoughts of acts way too sexy to perform in the next three minutes. "I know you're nervous. You don't have to be. It's going to work out."

I hope like hell he's right. "So, hot shot, where are you taking me tonight?"

"It's a surprise."

"You know I'm not a fan of surprises."

"I hope you like this one," he says as we dispose of the

sandwich wrappings and clean the bistro table. "I'm really excited."

That's obvious, and because he is, I tamp down my inherent cynicism. "I'm definitely interested to see what you've cooked up."

"Just...keep an open mind, okay?"

"Sure." Now that he's pried it open, I don't see another option anyway.

West kisses my knuckles. "We're leaving in an hour. And, um...wear something sexy and elegant but comfortable enough to spend a few minutes outdoors."

"Outdoors? Where are you taking me?"

With a grin, he palms his car keys. "You take a shower. I have one more errand to run. See you soon..."

WEST

My palms are sweating as we get closer to the Hotel Casa del Mar in Santa Monica. Arranging tonight took a lot of phone calls while Eryn slept. Thank god money can move mountains, or this idea would never have become reality on such short notice.

Now I just hope tonight is as special to Eryn as it is to me.

She looks absolutely stunning in a silky taupe-colored jumpsuit with spaghetti straps that bisect her delicate shoulders and crisscross her back before tapering to gather around her small waist, then flare into pants with wide legs that almost appear skirt-like until she walks. The look is perfect, just like she is.

When I flip on my blinker and slow down at the entrance

to the parking lot, she freezes. "Why are we coming here?"

"You don't like this place?"

"I do. It's just...this is where you proposed. What—"

"Deep breath. I've arranged for us to have dinner by the ocean."

My response calms her, and I try not to grimace. Eryn is willing to try working with me to build a future together again. But her anxiousness gives me pause. Am I doing the right thing?

I'm still not sure when the valet takes my car and I lead Eryn inside. Heads turn in her direction. I can't help but notice other appreciative male stares cast her way as I ask her to wait in a chair by the door.

On the other side of the lobby, the concierge smiles at my whispered request before he disappears down the hall. Less than two minutes later, a bald man in an impeccable tuxedo greets me.

I cross the room to claim Eryn again, then we follow the man to a lovely, familiar open-air restaurant/bar that faces the Pacific and has all the charm of Coastal Italy. Our host seats us and introduces himself, then leaves.

Eryn scans the oceanfront eatery. Candles flicker, giving the place a golden glow as sunset pours in, bright and warm. "There's no one else here."

"I reserved it exclusively for us."

Confusion tugs at her expression. "I don't understand."

She doesn't. Not yet. Of course she remembers that I proposed to her in this very restaurant. It was loud and crowded. I had to ask her twice, and she still never heard me over the din of weekend revelers. But me getting down on one knee and opening the ring box told her everything she needed to know. With a squeal and a nod, she jumped out of her chair and threw herself at me, tears filling her eyes. Then everyone clapped when I slid the ring on her finger. After that, at least half a dozen other patrons sent over drinks or bottles of champagne. We ended up spending the night at the hotel when we really couldn't afford it because we were too drunk to drive back to our little apartment. And we enjoyed every minute of the indulgent luxury and each other, certain of our future together.

That night was—and still is—one of my fondest memories.

But it occurs to me now that I have no idea whether it's one of hers or just a nightmare she'd rather forget.

I send her a smile, and I'm grateful a romantic instrumental begins to play softly from the overhead speakers, helping to set the mood. "Nothing to understand. I was in the mood for a little nostalgia."

She claps her mouth shut, but I can tell her thoughts are racing.

Before I can think of some way to fill the silence and set her at ease, a quiet waitress arrives to pour our water. She brings the cocktails and appetizers I preordered, then asks if there's anything else we need. After I glance at Eryn, who shrugs, I assure the woman we're fine. She melts away, giving us the privacy I insisted on. Dinner will only come when I tell them we're ready.

"West, what are we doing here? Really?"

"A lot of memories here, huh?"

Her stare skims over the one-hundred-eighty-degree views of the Pacific and Santa Monica pier a few blocks down the shoreline. "So many. This was always one of my favorite places. It's so beautiful. Of course I haven't been here since... you know."

"We were happy here."

Her face softens. "I don't think I've ever been happier in my life than I was that night."

Reaching across the table, I enfold her fingers with mine. "Same. But I realize now that every day I spend with you is one of the happiest days of my life. I didn't even know how miserable I was without you until I laid eyes on you again."

She glances down, not quite able to look my way with her pensive stare. "I always assumed you were happier without me. But I knew full well how miserable I felt."

"Is that why you were wearing your wedding dress and blitzed off bad wine the night I knocked on your door?"

"The vino wasn't that bad," she protests.

"By the smell of that crap, it wasn't good."

"All right. Maybe it sucked. But Echo brought it for me. She knew I'd had a rough day." Eryn taps her fingers on the table and drags in a nervous breath. "I woke up thinking of you that morning. I couldn't shake thoughts of you all day. I kept having this fantasy of seeing you again, but by the time I came home from Java and Jacks, I figured setting eyes on you was somewhere between unlikely and impossible, so I settled in with the merlot of dubious quality and donned my dress to pretend that it was our wedding day." She pauses, face turning pensive. "That's not the first time I've done it. As long as I could imagine walking down the aisle to you and forget our split, I was okay. As soon as reality crashed in... Well, you know how much I hate crying. But I often would. Then I'd hate myself for being delusional enough to think you'd ever come back and want me again."

"Oh, honey..."

"That's why, when I heard your voice that night, I was sure I had to be hallucinating. There was no way my dream of being with you again could possibly come true."

The pain in her voice breaks my heart. "If you were fantasizing about me, why were you so angry to see me?"

"Because you barged into my fantasy. The guy who hurt me, I mean. Not the West I fell in love with. I knew him. I didn't know the stranger undressing me with his stare. It probably sounds silly, but I was scared."

"I would never hurt you."

"Not physically, but emotionally... The moment I saw you again, I feared you still had the power to undo me. After thinking I was okay, other than my lacking sex life, it was a bitter pill. Then you wouldn't go away. And I sprawled on top of you. I remember thinking that being close to you felt so right. That only terrified me more."

For Eryn, that's a huge admission. In fact, she's been a lot braver with her feelings today than she was three years ago. I'm finally getting through to her, and she's not building walls between us. I'm proud of her. I don't say it because she won't want to hear that she's gone "soft," but her openness is definitely giving me hope for our future.

I squeeze her hand. "When we fell in your closet, it

didn't take feeling us pressed together for me to know that I couldn't let you get away a second time. I realized that the moment I set eyes on you."

Nervously, Eryn sips her cocktail, her stare never leaving mine. "You did?"

I nod. "I definitely couldn't deny it after I kissed you. The last week has only made me more sure."

Eryn doesn't say anything, but the telltale trembling of her chin and the sheen of unshed tears glossing her dark eyes speak volumes.

As the sun appears to dip into the big blue ocean, the lights of the Ferris wheel suddenly illuminate in the distance. Even the air around us seems to hold its breath.

It doesn't get any better than now, buddy...

Trying to calm my pounding heart, I fold my napkin on the table and stand. Eryn frowns in confusion as I approach and take her hands in mine. Then I kneel.

She gasps. "West?"

"I want to fix everything I broke three years ago. So... Eryn Rose Hope, say yes to marrying me again." I reach into my coat pocket and extract the velvet ring box I found in her nightstand. "Be my fiancée and wear this ring so we can finally be happy together for the rest of our lives."

She covers her gaping mouth and blinks at me. "You're serious?"

"Absolutely. I've never been more sure about anything. Be my wife. If you say yes and believe in us, I swear we'll make it to the altar."

"This is so sudden..."

"It's not," I argue. "We're continuing on where we left off before I let all the wrong things come between us. I still love you. I always have. I always will."

"But...you live in Vegas. I live in LA. Neither of us can just...move."

She's in shock more than actually questioning or protesting. It's in Eryn's skeptical nature to look at all sides of a situation and find the flaws.

"We'll work it out. If I have to move to LA..." I shrug. "I will. But maybe you'd be happier not getting up before the ass crack of dawn to work your butt off for twelve hours every day. Maybe you'll decide to go back to school after all. That's up to you. Either way, I'll do whatever I have to for us to be happy." I clear my throat. "But, um...any chance you could give me an answer? My knee isn't loving the hard tile."

She chokes out a laugh, her eyes bright with emotion. "Oh, my god. I might be crazy, but...yes." Tears squeeze from her eyes and roll down her face. "Yes."

Relief pours through me as I lunge for Eryn and grab her, pulling her tight against me. "I'm going to make you so happy, honey. I promise."

"I believe you'll try. And I'll do my best to make you happy, too."

I still hear that kernel of uncertainty. I don't think she distrusts me, but she's gun-shy. She doesn't trust the situation. Nothing but time and commitment will help her understand how much I mean every word I'm saying.

For now, I yank the ring out of its velvet case and toss the box onto the table. I'm not surprised to find myself trembling as I slide the simple white-gold band with a three-carat solitaire on her dainty finger. It still fits perfectly. And the diamond is still almost overwhelming on her petite hand. I send a silent thank-you upward to my grandfather for loaning me the money to buy this ring when I didn't have two pennies of my own to rub together.

"It's still the most beautiful ring I've ever seen." She watches the gemstone wink and sparkle on her finger. "I cried so hard when I took it off for good."

"You'll never have to do that again," I vow.

With one last glance at the diamond, she looks up at me. "I hope you're right, that nothing and no one can come between us again."

"We won't let it." I cup her face and bend for a kiss to seal us together. "You're going to make a wonderful Mrs. Weston Quaid."

She smiles before I seize her mouth for a tender kiss.

Behind me, I hear the small staff dedicated to our evening clapping, along with the pop of a champagne cork.

She laughs, breaking our kiss. "It's just like old times."

"What do you say we have dinner, get drunk, and make love all night here again?"

Eryn frowns. "I'd love to, but we didn't pack. And we don't have a room. Or...do we?"

My grin widens. "Actually, I did and we do. I didn't unpack my bag from Vegas. Neither did you. And I managed to get us a suite overlooking the ocean with a balcony. How about it?"

"Yes." She leans in to kiss me. "I can't believe we're here and that I'm trusting you, but yes to everything, especially our future. West..." She bites her lip. "I love you, too. I never stopped."

I hold Eryn closer and kiss her until she's breathless because I'm so damn happy. She loves me—and she's willing to tell me. That's *huge* for her. It took a long time for her to say the words when we first dated. Her whispered admission now proves her heart is involved, too, and that she's committed to making this work.

As I hold her close and press kisses along her jaw, I motion to our waiting server to bring dinner.

Though our surf and turf is delicious, neither one of us is focused on food. We down the champagne and get drunk off our longing glances at each other. Yeah, I can't wait to get her upstairs, peel her clothes off, and lay every inch of her body bare for me. Her flushed cheeks and bright eyes tell me she knows it.

I lift my glass to my fiancée, gratified to see her engagement ring winking on her finger as she toasts me in return. "To looking forward, not back. And to us."

"To us." She sips, then sets her glass aside. "Have you given any thought about when you want to get married? Next October fourth?"

Our original wedding day? "That's almost a year away. No."

"Too long to wait? How about June? I wouldn't hate being a summer bride. Maybe we could do something outdoors."

"Still too long. I was thinking more like next Saturday."

Eryn rears back. "That gives me less than a week to plan a wedding!"

"I've already waited three years for this, and I hate like hell that I have to wait until after the no-confidence vote my uncle Eddie is shoving on the board next Friday. After that, I don't want to wait anymore."

"He's still trying to oust you? Your father's own brother?"

I shrug. "I don't care about him. I should be able to weather this vote. But as soon as it's over, I intend to make you mine for good."

Her cheeks flush with her happy smile. "It's crazy, but okay. I have a wedding dress. I'll call my sisters. We'll figure out how to make it work... Where do we hold the ceremony? Getting a venue at the last minute..."

"Hey, last-minute weddings happen all the time in Vegas. Everything will be all right, honey. I'll help you. Don't stress."

She nods. "You're right. This is a happy occasion for us. The rest is just details."

"Exactly."

"We'll have to start tomorrow. Once we pick a time and place, we'll have to let friends and family know..." Her expression turns taut again. "Oh. What about your family?"

I wince. "At this point, I'm not inclined to invite anyone from my side except Gen and Flynn. But you need to meet my mother, then we can decide how to handle things. I also think it's critical for you to understand who you'll be up against and to show her that you won't bow to her bullying. If you don't, you'll never have a moment's peace in this marriage. She'll make sure of it."

"You really think she'll try to split us up again?"

"I don't think; I know." And it will be ugly, I have no doubt.

But tonight is for celebrating. I'll worry about Miriam Quaid later. This time, however, I'll be prepared. I know precisely how hard my mother will come gunning for Eryn. And I'll make sure that nothing and no one can drive a wedge between my former ex and me ever again.

CHAPTER NINE

On Wednesday night, I'm horrifically nervous as I prepare the dining room for the family dinner West and I are hosting so I can meet his family. I set the table with some china I found on clearance since West didn't have any. The wine glasses aren't crystal, but they're nice. I even found some linen napkins that coordinate well with everything. I didn't see the point of splurging on the matching placemats when West already had some made of sturdy bamboo.

Stepping back, I survey the results. Not exactly elegant... but not bad. Then again, this is an informal family dinner. Casual and easy, right? My mother always served everything she could on paper plates, so my extra touches elevate this meal to something above the ordinary.

So does the fact that West's mother will probably come looking for a way to tear us apart.

Shoving down my nerves, I glance at my watch. Twenty minutes until six? Holy crap. I barely have time to finish pulling myself together before everyone arrives at the top of the hour. And where is West? He said he'd be here by now.

The fact that he's worked late all week doesn't surprise

or bother me. I know the board vote is in two short days, and he probably has a mountain of work—and schmoozing—to accomplish in order to ensure the no-confidence vote goes his way. But he didn't roll in last night until almost nine. If he's late tonight, I'll have to face his mother alone. Not that I can't. I'm braced for her to launch a snide, vindictive attack. But I'd rather not have to fend her off by myself the first time we meet.

I send a quick text to West, asking if he's able to come home soon. No reply. Maybe he's driving? Stuck in traffic?

After dashing around the penthouse to finish cleaning up, I toss on my little black dress, fluff my hair, and touch my makeup. As I'm sliding into my shoes, I hear the doorbell ring.

Please be Flynn or Gen...

As I run for the door, I peek at my phone. Still no response from West. And whoever is knocking arrived ten minutes early.

Bracing myself with a breath, I pull the door open to find an unfamiliar man standing there, but I know instantly who he is. The family resemblance is too strong not to guess. "Hi. You must be West's Uncle Edward."

"I am." He scans me up and down. "And you must be my nephew's lay of the week. You know, if you want a rich and powerful man to fuck you, you could do better. Me, for example."

His words leave me gaping. They're slurred just enough to tell me he's been drinking. I was prepared for his mother to breathe fire on me like a she-dragon, but not for his uncle to proposition me. "I'm not his lay of the week. I'm—"

"Don't be a crass womanizer," a female voice cuts in from behind him, then a woman shoulders her way past the man, glaring at him as she saunters through the door. "She's not interested. Hi, I'm Miriam Quaid."

West's mother. My heart starts pounding. I'm alone with the two most hostile people in his family.

She turns to me, her pale hair arranged into an elegant twist. Her ice-blue dress clings to her slender form and matches her eyes perfectly.

Trying to stay calm, I extend my hand. "Nice to meet you, Mrs. Quaid. I'm Eryn Hope."

"The ex-fiancée?" As we shake, she glances at my free hand and spies my engagement ring. If she has any reaction, she's good at hiding it. "Or maybe not so ex anymore?"

I don't comment. West and I planned this dinner to announce our engagement together. "Come in. Your son isn't home from work yet."

Miriam enters and glances around the penthouse. "Just as well. I think you and I should chat first anyway."

I steady myself. Here comes whatever adversarial crap the woman has up her sleeve.

"Drink?" I offer.

"No, thank you."

"Don't talk to her. She'll rip you apart, girl," Eddie offers, helping himself to whatever booze West has in a decanter on the far edge of the living room. Once it's filled, he lifts his glass. "Mark my words."

"Don't be so dramatic," she snaps, then cups my shoulder. "Let's step onto the patio, where we can talk in peace."

The thought of being alone with her makes me uneasy. Where is West? Another surreptitious glance at my phone proves he hasn't returned my text.

As soon as she opens the slider to the patio, a gust of cool, dry air greets me. When we step out, the sun has nearly set. The lights of the Strip begin to brighten and flash as I lead her to a couple of plush patio chairs by a banked fire pit.

"This looks comfortable." Miriam sits. "And Eddie won't bother us here. As sloshed as he is—I hope he didn't drive here—he'll likely pass out before dinner. That would make the evening much more pleasant."

"Thank you for putting your brother-in-law in his place. I'm grateful. Has he always been this way?"

It really shouldn't be my first question or concern, but based on everything West has told me, I can't help but worry the man is drinking himself to death.

"An irresponsible alcoholic? For as long as I've known him, yes. He failed his father's expectations too many times as a youth, and once Hanover passed away... Well, I guess discovering he wasn't the favorite remaining heir was too bitter a pill for Edward to swallow without liquid assistance."

It's a biting observation, but it echoes what West said.

And I really shouldn't let myself be distracted. The woman has cornered me for a reason. Letting my guard down could be disastrous. I also intend to lead the conversation. The best defense is a good offense. Dad always said that was true in investigative journalism. My experience has proven it's true in life, too.

"So...what do you want to talk about? My relationship with your son? I know you don't approve, but you can't split us up again. Nothing will come between us this time."

She rears back in shock. "Is that what he told you? That I didn't want him to marry you?"

I choose my words carefully. "He said you threatened to tell me that he'd romanced me to dissuade my dad from doing an exposé about Quaid Enterprises so I'd call off the wedding."

She blinks as if it's obvious I'm missing the big picture. "I didn't threaten to tell you in order to break you up. I merely contended that any woman he married deserved to know the truth before you exchanged I do's. And that if he didn't do the decent thing and tell you, I would. I'm presuming you would have wanted to know."

I would, and her explanation makes sense. Still... "According to West, you wanted him to marry someone you chose."

Miriam shakes her head. "I told him it would be nice to at least meet you before the wedding so I could shake your hand and welcome you into the family. But West didn't want me 'interfering' with his scheme, so I wasn't invited. Then, Hanover collapsed and fell into a coma, West rushed home, and the wedding never happened. The truth is..." She sends me a soft, empathetic glance. "He said he'd changed his mind about marrying you. I'm guessing he never told you that."

Her version of events is so different from West's. I don't know what to say. Is she contorting the events to suit her narrative? Maybe, but her explanation also makes sense. Is it possible West misrepresented his mother's intentions so he wouldn't look like the bad guy? I don't want to believe it...

"He said you sent him on a date with another woman the week after we split up because you didn't approve of me."

"How could I possibly disapprove of someone I knew almost nothing about?"

"So you didn't want West to marry a woman with a blue-blood, East Coast pedigree?"

She looks stunned by my question. "I wanted a daughter-in-law, not a show dog. Lindsay, the girl in the photo, is the daughter of one of Quaid Enterprises' board members. When West announced that he'd decided not to marry you, he asked me to introduce him to her. I did because I hoped he would settle down and stop the busy revolving door to his bedroom. Instead, he exploited her soft heart to help persuade the board to give him interim control of the company after Hanover's death. I was horrified." She shakes her head. "There isn't anything my son wouldn't do for Quaid Enterprises. You've figured that out, I hope."

I gape. Though he admitted to seducing me to help smooth the company's way during their transition in the LA market, it never occurred to me that he might do the same to someone else.

"I'm sorry if I'm shocking you." She lays her warm hand over mine. "I told West he should at least do you the courtesy of ending the engagement before debauching Lindsay, but he's like his father. My husband was also only ever loyal to Quaid Enterprises. Everything and everyone else... Well, I was aware of Kingston's shortcomings as a husband. Even though it made me a fool, I still loved him."

Miriam knew her husband was unfaithful and accepted it? I blink in shock. I would care—very much. The West I know would, too. He doesn't seem like the sort to fuck around for a cheap thrill. He was never unfaithful when we were engaged in the past. But her charge of West using his good looks and his prowess in bed to further the company hits a little too close to home for me not to listen.

I swallow a lump in my throat. My stomach turns.

This woman is my enemy, I remind myself. She's probably twisting everything around to suit her purposes, and I refuse to second-guess my commitment to West based on anything she says. He swore she'd come at me. I assumed that would be a straightforward, full-frontal assault. Perhaps she's simply being more underhanded. It's her word against West's, and I'm siding with the man I plan to marry.

What if you're being naïve because you want to believe in him and your happily ever after so badly?

I shove the voice down and regard my future mother-in-law. "Thank you for your explanation. I'll keep all that in mind."

Miriam squeezes my hand. "You seem like a very nice girl. You clearly have feelings for my son, and as a mother, I want that for West. But I also don't want to see you disillusioned. You may not know this, but if Kingston hadn't died flying that silly plane of his, I intended to leave him. I thought the sex between us would be good forever. And if not, at least I would have money—something I hadn't grown up with. But I soon found out that there wasn't enough money in the world for me to overlook his transgressions."

"I'm not interested in money."

"Oh, I'm not implying you are. I'm simply worried about you. How will you feel when you hear about or see West with other women? How will you deal when you're hosting a party and have to welcome his mistress as a guest in your home because she's someone who can open doors for Quaid Enterprises? That happened to me more than once. It wasn't easy to cope with. So before you say 'I do,' think long and hard about the pitfalls of being Mrs. Weston Quaid. I love my son, and if you genuinely believe you can live with his flaws, then by all means, marry him." Suddenly, she pastes on a smile. "Listen to me. I sound like Doubting Debbie. I don't mean to dissuade you. Let's talk about happier things. Have you set a wedding date?"

"Saturday."

And I'm beyond stressed. We found a chapel to host the event. Unfortunately, it's next door to a 7-Eleven, but it's the best we could get last minute. The day we agreed to the venue, the only thing that mattered was being West's wife.

Now, I hate to admit it, but I'm having second thoughts.

Miriam gasps. "He's not giving you a lot of time to think this through, is he? But you love him. I hope very much that I'm wrong about everything and that your marriage is the fairy tale you've always imagined. If I could give you one piece of womanly—dare I say, maternal—advice, I would urge you to watch him for the next few days. Now that I've told you the truth, look at your relationship through that lens. Talking to him won't do any good. Every one of those Quaid men, my own sons included, are silver-tongued devils. They know how to say exactly what you want to hear."

Miriam stands. Head racing, I follow suit. I have no idea what to think, but I'm reeling. My chest hurts. God, I want her to be lying about all of it.

"Thank you," I manage to say.

She smiles. "My pleasure. Shall we see if—"

"Eryn?" I turn to find West standing in the patio door, eyes pinned on me, his expression concerned.

Irrational relief fills me. Somehow, he's going to put me at ease. Everything will be all right. "Hi."

"Mother?" he drawls.

"Is that any proper way to greet us? Come over here and give your lovely fiancée a kiss."

Scowling, he approaches us slowly, scanning my face as though he's trying to read my thoughts. I'm shell-shocked, and I suspect it shows.

As he draws closer and stands under the patio lights, I notice that West is flushed and sweaty. And he's very definitely late.

"Where have you been?"

"I had a meeting with Olivia Martin. She's on the board. It ran long, and when I got here, the elevator was broken. So I walked up forty flights of stairs. It took a while."

"Olivia?" his mother drawls. "Oh, Paul Martin's widow. She's so young and beautiful. What a tragedy. I hope she won't be alone for long. She must be so lonely... But you're merely interested in her vote. I'm sure she'll give it to you."

My heart seizes up. West was holed up all afternoon with someone's pretty young widow? I don't want to distrust him, but the elevator story seems thin. That sucker was working twenty minutes ago. Sure, it might stop functioning at any time, but...what are the odds?

What if West has an entirely different reason for being winded and red-faced? One that involves doing the horizontal tangle with a board member days before the no-confidence vote?

Eddie stumbles out onto the patio. "What kind of piss is this Scotch, boy?"

West turns, and the moment is broken as he tries to good-naturedly defend his brand of booze.

"Excuse me. I need to check on dinner," I murmur to make my escape to the kitchen.

West tries to follow me inside, but the doorbell rings again. With a curse, he veers off to admit his brother and sister. And it seems the elevator is magically working again...

I don't know how I make it through the uncomfortable dinner. I manage to smile in the right places and act engaged in the conversation, even happy when Gen and Flynn congratulate us on our upcoming wedding. I feel nothing but a weeping hole of confusion and anguish seeping in my chest. I want to ask West for an explanation almost as badly as I'm worried whatever he says will be a lie.

This is one time I'm thankful for the role of hostess, so I can use clearing the table and starting coffee as an escape from West's prying gaze. The minute he ushers his family out, I run, fleeing to my bathroom before shutting and locking the door.

Moments later, West pounds on it. "Eryn, what did my mother say to you? Don't tell me nothing. I know better."

"I'm tired," I lie because I need to think this through. "I'm getting a migraine."

"Honey, don't shut me out. Let's talk about this."

"There's nothing to say." I flip on the shower to drown him out.

He curses and punches the door as he storms away.

I hide in the bathroom with my iPad for almost three hours. I leave pleading texts for both Echo and Ella, who are arriving tomorrow for the wedding.

It's after one a.m. when I finally venture into the bedroom to find West sprawled across the bed, illuminated by the muted light on the nightstand, looking so gorgeous and male in nothing but a pair of boxer briefs. I ache to talk to him, ask him to hold me and make all my doubts go away. But I can't. I really should observe him as impartially as possible over the next few days and decide for myself—without his well-placed words and panty-melting lovemaking crowding out my protests—whether he's the love of my life or a lying snake I need to purge from my heart. And I need to decide in the next two days, before I say "I do."

WEST

I don't know exactly what's upset Eryn, but I know my mother is behind it.

The next day, I'm distracted at the office when I can't afford to be. The board's vote of no confidence is tomorrow. True, Uncle Eddie shouldn't be a threat...if the board members are being objective. But my meeting with Olivia Martin last night proved very interesting. Apparently, my father's playboy younger brother has been "comforting" the widow for the past two weeks. And when he pushed her to vote for him, it finally occurred to her why he'd been so "helpful" lately.

After a lot of embarrassment and a few tears, I produced spreadsheets to show her the improvements in our bottom line, particularly in the last six months. Since Olivia is a social creature, she attends events and galas with a lot of the other board members. She helped me hone tomorrow's presentation to address the others' concerns about my youth and lack of experience. She has my eternal gratitude, and I think the vote is more likely to be favorable now that I can address specific objections. So I couldn't rush Olivia out the door when she needed to talk about what a douche my uncle is. And especially when she divulged the creative, despicable ways he's been trying to woo votes. Then I arrived at my complex to find the freaking elevator not functioning...

Obviously, Eryn was alone with my mother far too long.

All through dinner last night she looked pale and shaken. She sent me glances both startled and accusing.

What the fuck did my mother say? I have no idea, and Eryn isn't talking.

She also won't let me close enough to kiss her.

As I step off the elevator at my condo complex, I rake a hand through my hair. I had every intention of coming home early so my fiancée and I could talk things out, but I received some new financials that were too good not to put into tomorrow's presentation. So more than three hours later, I'm late—again.

When I open the front door, I find a small crowd. Eryn is there, avoiding my stare with an expression that's both angry and sad. Echo flanks her on one side, looking boho chic with her long brownish hair arranged in a complicated mix of twists, braids, and wavy tresses that cascade down her back. Her slender form is draped in flowing lace and Birkenstocks. On her other side, Ella stands in a muted-pink wraparound shirt, black slacks, and kitten heels.

Her sisters both look at me like I'm the devil.

Fuck.

On the other side of the room, two men stand, looking out the windows at my view of the Strip. They couldn't be more opposite. One wears an impeccable suit. The other sports black sweat pants with a matching zip-up jacket, a gray shirt, and athletic shoes.

"Carson?" Ella calls.

The suit turns, then catches my gaze and smiles.

I send one last look at Eryn—yep, still avoiding me—then step forward to meet this guy. "You must be Ella's new husband. I'm Weston Quaid. Just call me West."

"Carson Frost. Nice to meet you. I've heard a lot about you." His face says most of it isn't good.

"Nice to meet you, too."

The guy dressed like a jock saunters closer. He's a couple of years younger than me. As tall and solidly as he's built, it's obvious he's been an athlete most of his life. "Hayes Elliot."

"Glad you're here. You're Echo's...boyfriend?"

He looks across the room at her with a frown, then shakes his head. "No, her best friend. We've been super tight since we were, like, seven."

The two don't appear to have anything in common. Hayes looks like a traditional college campus man, complete with stockbroker haircut and fashionable five-o'clock shadow. Echo looks as if someone plucked her out of a *Vogue* circa 1971. But when Eryn's younger sister sends Hayes a sunny smile, he gives her a head lift and a grin back.

They aren't romantic? Because that's the vibe I'm getting...

Then I see what must be Hayes's duffel and a hanging bag containing his suit draped across the sofa.

"You don't mind if I sleep here, do you?" he asks. "I gave Echo the bedroom."

It's on the tip of my tongue to say that maybe they should try sharing it, but it's none of my business and I have bigger problems. "Absolutely. No worries. I should say hello to my bride since I'm so late. Everyone has eaten, right?"

"Yeah," Carson assures me, then grabs my arm. "Why don't you show us this view on the patio for a minute?"

Man-speak for "let's talk." I met this guy five minutes ago. I can't imagine what he has to say to me, but I shrug. "All right."

I cast Eryn one last glance, which she still doesn't meet, before the three of us step outside. The dry, cool wind hits my face as we look out over the familiar lights brightening the night sky.

"What's up?" I ask Carson. Hayes seems more detached from the situation.

"You tell me. Eryn doesn't seem like a happy bride."

"My mother got a hold of her last night and said... something. Eryn won't tell me what. Do you know anything?"

Both guys shake their heads.

"I'll work on Ella," Carson assures me.

"Echo might confide in me," Hayes offers. "She does that a lot since, you know, I'm not a 'threat' or whatever."

"Thanks. I've been racking my brain, but my mother... There's no telling what she's said or done."

After a pair of nods, it's clear they're not sure whether to believe or trust me, but they're willing to give me the benefit of the doubt—at least until I screw up. For the next few minutes, I point out different hotels and attractions, talk about upcoming changes to the view, and invite them to have a drink. Both decline, and we wander back inside.

I'm immediately drawn to Eryn. I can't not be close to her. Not knowing what she thinks I'm guilty of is killing me. Actually, knowing she suspects I'm guilty of anything at all hurts most.

As I march across the room, Ella tries to intercept me, smiling as she puts her body protectively between Eryn and me. "Hi, West. It's been a long time. Why don't we catch up?"

I bypass her with a sharp shake of my head. "I need to talk to my fiancée, and you know it."

"Actually, I don't think you do."

"With all due respect, this is between Eryn and me. I appreciate that you're being a protective older sister, but now I intend to be the concerned husband-to-be. Excuse me."

I no more than pass Ella up when Echo intercepts me. "She needs girl time."

The hippie chick has steel in her eyes. But it's nothing compared to my resolve.

"Not as much as she needs to hear my mother can be a lying bitch." I nudge her aside. "Excuse me."

As I approach Eryn, she lifts her chin and finally looks at me. Her eyes flare. I see tears form.

She turns and darts down the hall. Maybe I should care who's watching this drama play out. I don't. I have no idea what's going on. And that needs to stop.

The slamming of the door tells me she's retreated to her bathroom—the one place I'm not supposed to violate her privacy.

Goddamn it.

The snick of the lock sets off all my instincts.

"Open the door, Eryn."

"No."

"Open the fucking door so you can tell me what's going on and I can explain."

"There's nothing to say."

I hear the catch in her voice. She's crying.

"The hell there isn't."

I'm past caring if this will cost me ten thousand dollars and a new door. I kick the damn thing open. Wood splinters. The knob bangs off the opposite wall. The heavy wooden slab hangs lopsided from one hinge.

And Eryn stands before me looking devastated.

My chest seizes up as I rush to her side and grab her shoulders. "Whatever my mother told you, it isn't true."

She dips her head. "I want to believe that, but..."

"But she made it sound good. I know. She has a talent for twisting the truth for her own purposes, but whatever bullshit she fed you on a silver platter...it's still bullshit, honey." When Eryn doesn't respond, I sigh. "Let me guess, I don't really love you, according to her."

She nods.

"Am I cheating, too?"

Eryn hesitates. "Probably."

"Of course. And?" Silence. "What else? I can't tell you all the ways she's wrong if I don't even know what she's accused me of."

"I need to figure out what's real and what's not on my own. And I need to decide what happens next."

Next? Whether or not Eryn is going to marry me? The possibility she might not terrifies me.

"You do." I want to pull her close so badly, it hurts. But Eryn isn't braced for that, and she'll only resist me. "But if you're going to make up your mind, shouldn't you hear both sides of the story?"

Slowly, she lifts her head. I hold my breath, waiting, until our stares meet. There's that *zing* between us. Of course I see her hurt and confusion, but nothing dilutes our chemistry.

"Thank you," I breathe. "Now tell me... Who am I cheating with?"

"Olivia Martin. But in the future, it could be any woman who's in a position to help you and Quaid Enterprises get ahead."

Immediately, I see the tactic my mother took. She used my history with Eryn to create a narrative that feeds all of my fiancée's worst insecurities.

"I've never touched that woman. Olivia Martin is a board member. She came by my office..."

Over the next ten minutes, I explain everything, including the fact that Uncle Eddie has been consoling her horizontally in the hopes of getting her vote tomorrow.

"All right. But why were you late tonight?"

"The latest financial data came in, and it was too good not to include in my presentation. I was in my office alone. You could have called. I would have answered. I would have assured you that I love you. Only you."

Eryn's expression says she's hearing me...but she's afraid to believe. On the one hand, it's frustrating that she's still so mistrustful. On the other, I've worked past her prickly outer shell to the real woman she hides underneath. I'm seeing the broken, scared parts of her she never wants anyone to see. That she's willing to be vulnerable with me says she hasn't totally convicted me in her mind. If she had, she would have already packed and left.

Thank god I still have a chance.

"Honey, ask yourself this: why would I have tried so hard to win you back if I didn't love you? If you weren't the woman I want to spend my life with? If I only wanted someone who could help me or the company get ahead?"

Finally, she blinks and softens. "I kept asking myself that question. It's the one thing that stopped me from breaking our engagement and leaving. But you can care about someone and still cheat."

With a clench of my jaw, I shake my head. "Maybe other guys can. Hell, maybe my father even did. Is that what my mother told you?"

"Yeah. She said like father, like son."

Clenching my fists, I try to count to ten and hold my tongue. There aren't enough curse words in the English language to adequately reflect my fury right now. "I was young when my dad died, so maybe it's true. But I am *not* him. I wouldn't do that to you. And we've come too far to let my conniving mother come between us again. Did she also tell you that our past breakup was none of her doing?"

Eryn nods.

"Yeah, she's a saint." I shake my head, anger so close to bubbling over. But I have to continue tamping it down and focus on the woman in front of me, the one I want to love forever. The bitch I wish I could strangle right now will have to wait. "And she somehow made me out to be the lying dirtbag because I didn't tell you the real reason we started dating, right?"

"Well, you didn't."

"I own up to that. But my mother wasn't in the truth-and-virtue camp either, I promise. The only reason she wanted to tell you was because she hoped it would split us apart. If not for that, if she had approved of you as a daughter-in-law, she wouldn't have given two shits about being honest with you. She would have smiled at the wedding and tried to be your best fucking friend so she could manipulate and control you. Don't be fooled by her pretty face and innocent act."

"Everything she said made so much sense, West. I—"

"Of course it did. She thought about what she wanted to say before she arrived, and I can almost guarantee it was rehearsed. My mother may seem quiet and ladylike. She can even pull off kind and supportive when she's really motivated. But she's like a snake. She sheds her 'friendly' skin and turns into a slithering viper when there's money and power involved."

Eryn looks away pensively. "I don't know what to think.

I didn't want to believe anything she said...but for every objection I had, she—"

"Had a perfectly logical explanation for why she's right and I'm an asshole. Honey, she's only trying to come between us again. Please don't let her."

"I need to think tonight. Be alone."

That's the last thing Eryn needs.

"I've given you time to yourself, and you're only more confused and upset." Finally, I take her in my arms. She's stiff... but she allows me against her body. "Why didn't you just talk to me?"

"Because I want to believe everything you say, and I thought if I watched you and observed, really paid attention to your actions, the truth would become clear."

"And it isn't. Because the vote is tomorrow, I've put in a lot of hours at the office this week. That's stressed you more because the wedding is in thirty-six hours, which didn't leave you a lot of time to decide what to do. Not knowing if you'll be speaking vows to me on Saturday or packing your bags and leaving is tearing you up, right?"

"Something like that."

"Wait here." I kiss her forehead, then dash back through our bedroom and fling open the door.

Everyone is congregated a few feet away, like they're waiting for us to emerge. At my sudden appearance, the low tones of their conversation fall immediately silent.

"Does anyone need anything else tonight?" I ask them.

No one says a word.

"Look, help yourself to whatever is in the refrigerator.

If you want something substantial, there's a great restaurant downstairs. Menu is in the first drawer in the kitchen. Put it on my tab. There's booze in the bar, the TV remote is on the coffee table, and Hayes, there are blankets and pillows in the closet in Echo's room. I'll be with Eryn, and we'd appreciate some privacy."

Ella steps forward. "But my sister—"

"Is mine right now. Good night." I shut the door.

That makes me a terrible host, but repairing my relationship with Eryn is way more important than being polite.

When I turn, Eryn is behind me, arms wrapped around her middle. God, I can't stand to see her like this. She's never looked so torn, defeated.

Fuck this. I refuse to let my mother win again.

Suddenly, it doesn't matter that I haven't eaten in seven hours and I really want a hot shower. I want Eryn happy way more. My own comfort can wait.

"Come here, honey. Let me hold you."

She approaches—slowly, with small steps, swallowing down her nerves.

"I won't hurt you," I assure her.

"Maybe you won't mean to." She blinks up at me, and I see worry and strained hope teeter-tottering on her face.

God, she has such a hard time believing people won't shit on her. I could blame her absent parents—and I kind of do— but I have to blame myself, too. She went out on a limb and believed in me three years ago. And I flushed all her trust away. Now my shrewd mother is using my stupidity and Eryn's own skepticism to drive us apart.

I cup my bride-to-be's face. "I won't at all. Ever. I'm going to be here, be yours, and be faithful. I promise."

When I risk kissing her, she doesn't shy away. A glide of my lips over hers turns into another. Then another. And another still.

Her little whimper tells me she's reeling, perched on the precipice of surrender. I hold her tighter and whisper, "I love you, honey. So, so much."

Finally, Eryn melts against me and throws her arms around me. Her tears flow as I slowly lay her down, peel her clothes away, and assure her with my words and my body that there's no other woman for me and I will never let anyone come between us again.

When I finish making love to Eryn, she's clinging and sobbing, silently conveying how confused she's been and how contrite she feels. I kiss her, reassure her again. I hope she wakes up tomorrow determined—happy, even—to marry me on Saturday. But I'm worried she may still be worried and wary, that we're in danger of hitting a dead end.

I hold her against me until she drifts off, but sleep eludes me.

Finally, I throw on a pair of sweat pants, grab my phone, and head to the kitchen. Carson and Ella have retired for the night. Echo and Hayes are sitting in front of my big screen, watching a Thursday night football game. Her head is on his beefy shoulder. He's wrapped his arm around her petite frame. Their body language is speaking volumes, and I wonder why neither of them seems to be hearing it.

I grab a protein bar, some baby carrots, and a bottle of water, then stalk to my office, shut the door, and wolf some down as I dial my mother. It's after eleven, and she's probably in bed. I don't give a shit.

She answers on the first ring. "West. It's good to hear from you."

"Drop the act. Eryn isn't with me to hear it. What the fuck is wrong with you? I love this woman, and you seem determined to screw me out of marrying her again. Why? Because you didn't choose her?"

Miriam laughs. "Nothing like that. Though it would have been nice if you had consulted me."

"Why would I ask my mommy who I can marry?"

"Because I have better taste than you, clearly."

Her answer sets my teeth on edge. "Eryn is perfect."

"You're blinded by lust. I guess that means she's a good lay. Probably creative in bed, too. I'm sure those trailer-park girls are. But I assure you, she's not perfect. Even Olivia Martin, whom I really don't like, would be a better choice. At least she could bring *something* to the marriage."

"I'm not marrying Eryn for her money or connections."

"Obviously."

"That's not what's most important."

"How naïve of you to think so. You were born into a life of diamonds and champagne. Eryn comes from pennies and beer. Please think bigger and better."

"You saying she's not good enough for me?"

"That should be apparent, even to you. That table she set for dinner was a joke, West, and you know it. Olivia is only thirty-one, but if you'd like a younger, more suitable wife, James Warren's daughter just turned twenty. That would help shore up a vote you're missing on the board. And Blair is very sweet. Attending Vassar. She'll inherit lots of money. Marrying her could open doors for both you and the company. I bet she's a virgin, so if you like that kind of thing—"

"You're vile. What I want with Eryn is a marriage, not a business transaction. And I have nothing more to say to you until after the wedding. I know you'll vote for me tomorrow because it's in your own financial interest. Uncle Eddie would only scheme to get you off the board and out of his hair once and for all. I won't—unless you force my hand. In return, don't you dare speak another word to Eryn until I give my permission. And Mom, that may be never."

CHAPTER TEN

ERYN

"Morning, honey," West murmurs as he kisses me awake. As my lashes flutter open, he's above me with a smile. "Hi."

"Sleep well?"

Fitful dreams. Nagging worries.

"Decent," I lie. "You?"

"I always sleep better beside you." He brushes his lips across my forehead. "I have to get ready for this circus—I mean board meeting—but when I come home...it will be our last night as singles. I think Ella and Echo have some sort of bachelorette party planned. And I'm pretty sure Flynn wants to get me shitfaced." He rolls his eyes. "Don't forget to pick up your wedding dress from the dry cleaner this morning."

"I did that Wednesday afternoon," I answer automatically.

"Excellent. I can't wait to see you wearing it again, this time as you come down the aisle to be my wife." With a last kiss to my cheek, he eases out of bed and heads toward the *his* bathroom on the left side of the master suite. I rise and head for the massive closet in the palatial *hers*.

Insecurity still plagues me this morning. I can't seem to quash all my fears, and I don't understand why. West and

I talked last night. He made love to me tenderly. Afterward, I felt a lot better about us. In fact, I felt sure he loves me and would never hurt me. But when he rolled away to sleep and I closed my eyes, all the doubts came tumbling back.

I hate sounding like an anxious, overdramatic teenage girl worried about whether the cute guy at school likes her. I need to put this mistrust behind me. What else could West possibly do to prove that he loves and wants to marry me?

I'm not sure, but I already know logic isn't going to bury my niggling worries. Maybe our last wedding is haunting me. Three years ago, the day before our nuptials, I thought—with the exception of West's grandfather having cancer—that everything was perfect. Now, barely more than thirty hours before we're supposed to exchange I do's again, I'm nervous as hell. I keep waiting for the other shoe to drop. In the back of my head, I wonder if I'm making a mistake.

After sliding into some yoga pants and a T-shirt, I brush my teeth and head to the kitchen for coffee. Echo and Hayes are on the patio, laughing about something. For years, I've been waiting for them to realize they're more than friends. But no. Hayes continues to date a string of skanks, and Echo goes on pretending to be really into skateboarders with a cause. Neither of them ever seems to be in a serious relationship, and I have to wonder why neither looks at what's right in front of them.

As my brew drips from the machine, Ella heads straight for me and wraps me in a hug. "Are you okay?"

"Fine."

"West seemed angry last night."

"Not at me."

"Oh. Good. Did you two get everything worked out?"

I shrug. "Maybe."

"That's not a good response, considering the wedding is tomorrow. Do you want to marry him?"

"Yes. But only slightly more than I worry he'll someday break my heart. I know he loves me...in his way. I just don't know if that's enough. He's always going to be rich and in the spotlight. There will always be women willing to sleep with him for money or their fifteen minutes in the tabloids. Quaid Enterprises will always be toward the top of his priority list because he's ambitious and thousands of people rely on him to make the company super profitable. He'll always be the golden boy born with the silver spoon, and I'll always be the latchkey kid from the strictly middle-class neighborhood. Given all that...are we a recipe for disaster?"

"I think you two will be great. But you need to decide what you're going to do quickly. The big day is tomorrow, and—"

"Says the woman who was deciding whether or not to marry her husband as she walked down the aisle."

Ella shoots me a self-deprecating grin. "Do as I say, little sister, not as I do."

"Nice." I pick up the cup of coffee that's finally finished brewing. "In my shoes, what would you do?"

"Take a chance." She shrugs. "First, it worked for me. Second, if you don't, if you call it off this time, he won't come back. And I think you'll always wonder, what if..."

Yeah, I've considered that, too. I'm just not convinced it's a good enough reason to pledge my life to someone. I take promises seriously. Divorce isn't something I ever want to experience myself. Obviously, no one does, but growing up I told myself I'd only marry if I was madly in love and truly believed it would last forever.

Well, I'm madly in love...but I'm not convinced West and I are destined for eternity. Half of the equation is up to him, and all his pretty words aside, I don't know if he's being honest. After all, he hasn't always been honest with me. What if he can't put our marriage first once the vows have been spoken?

My sister and I fall silent when Carson emerges from the spare bedroom, kisses his wife, and starts his own coffee. Echo and Hayes dash inside, both looking for a java refill. Conversation about the day starts in earnest. I have a mani-pedi scheduled today, a consult with a makeup artist and hairdresser. And I have to call my parents to tell them I'm getting married. Until now, we've kept the event quiet. First, so it didn't leak to the press. Now because...what if I get cold feet?

As we're talking through the coming day—and the impromptu parties tonight—West jaunts out of the bedroom, an impeccable suit hugging his fine form perfectly.

He drops a kiss on my cheek as he grabs a protein bar and a coffee to go. "I'll be home about four. You should be done with all your appointments then, right?"

I nod. Irrationally, I'm worried that the closer I get to this man the more attached I become, but all I want to do is fling myself against him and beg him to hold me close. "Yeah."

"Then we'll all have a nice dinner before Flynn, Carson, Hayes, and I find some mischief on the Strip." He turns to Ella. "What do you have planned?"

She grins. "An evening full of dollar bills and sweaty, half-naked men."

"I didn't need to hear that, sweetheart," Carson grouses.

Hayes steps in front of his best friend protectively. "Echo doesn't like loud, dirty places full of strangers."

She elbows him. "I'll make an exception for this." At Hayes's scowl, she shrugs. "What's the worst that could happen? I'll be with my sisters."

West kisses me one more time. "As long as you wake up ready to be Mrs. Weston Quaid tomorrow, I'll be the happiest bastard alive."

His words touch me. I tell myself to drown the anxiety and doubt once and for all. But no, it's still sitting on my chest. I feel myself staring at him longingly, like this is the last time we'll ever be together, close.

"I hope the meeting goes well," I manage to get out.

"Thanks. I'm as prepared as I can be. I've got a strong voting bloc. And if Eddie turns up sober, I'll be shocked. If he doesn't, that will help my case. Except for the people whose asses he's licked or he's paid off, I should get the votes. Then this shit will be off my chest once and for all. And tomorrow, we'll celebrate by getting married, right?" He leans in for one last kiss and searches my face. "Have a good day, honey."

After he's gone, everyone pitches in to help cook some breakfast and do the dishes. My sisters and I get ready and bustle out the door.

A few hours later, I have blushing pink nails and toes, a face brightened by polished but tasteful makeup, and a romantic updo I absolutely love. Tomorrow, I'll want exactly the same look before the ceremony. Then we grab a fast-food lunch and hit the mall for a new party dress for tonight.

It's not quite two in the afternoon when we step off the penthouse's elevator. I'm laughing and feeling almost happy again. The minute we step inside the entryway, Carson and Hayes greet us with all the levity of a funeral procession.

"What's wrong?" I ask, my belly clenching with worry.

The two men look at one another, then Carson whips out his phone and sets it in front of me. "This hit the press fifteen minutes ago." Pity transforms his expression. "I'm sorry."

TMZ. There's a headline that stops my heart.

PLAYBOY CEO DISHING OUT FAVORS
FOR A FAVORABLE VOTE?

The picture below shows a man and a woman naked and entwined in a conference room, their lips plastered together as he lays her back on the table and covers her body with his own. The room is shadowed, and the picture is a bit grainy... but I'd know that profile anywhere. The date and time stamp says this image was captured two days ago, when West was late from work, didn't answer his phone, and arrived sweating and obviously exerted.

The summary identifies my fiancé and Olivia Martin and speculates that West must really want to keep his CEO chair to seduce the widow who inherited her late husband's board seat.

I shove the phone away, swallowing down both shock and tears.

"What do you want to do?" Ella asks gently.

My first instinct is to pack and leave. Right now, I don't

care if that nullifies our mistress pact and I end up broke, losing my restaurant, and on my ass financially. I want away from this man and all the pain that comes with him.

On the other hand, I'm furious. I want to understand his deception. Why the hell did he want to marry me so badly if he only intended to hurt me in the end?

"I'm staying. The second that asshole walks through the door, I suggest you all leave. It's going to get ugly. Then...you can take me home."

WEST

Could this meeting be any more ridiculous? There's a lot of unnecessary pomp and blustering before we get down to brass tacks. Uncle Eddie insists on speaking first. He makes his case, sounding almost sober. To someone not familiar with his ways, he probably doesn't seem under the influence at all. But I hear the slight hesitations, the silent lapses in speech while he gathers his words and thoughts.

His case is decently thought out but unfortunately not much different than the argument he made the last time he tried to take the CEO position from me—and failed.

Normally, I would suspect that my mother's acidic smile is merely smug acknowledgment that her brother-in-law is toast, but I don't like that look in her eyes. I like the way she keeps watching her phone even less.

Finally, it's my turn to talk.

Assuming the front of the conference room with confidence, I welcome everyone, look my adversaries in the eye, and challenge them to look at the results I've produced since assuming the CEO role and vote in the company's best interest rather than their own.

I'm only on the second slide—the one that shows the latest year-to-date financials—when my phone starts buzzing in my pocket. It buzzes again less than five seconds later. Then again. And again until it's a nonstop distraction.

With a curse, I pull it from my pocket to shut it off—then pause when I see a screen full of notifications. News articles, Instagram, Google notifications, and a mountain of texts. The first one I read at the top is from my sister. Gen wants to know if I've lost my mind and what I'm going to do now that the shit has hit the fan.

I freeze. What the hell is she talking about?

I glance up at my mother. Her smile couldn't be more smug.

"Carry on," she insists with a dismissive hand gesture and a placid mien that sets off all my warning bells.

What has she done to me? No, to Eryn.

I was a fool to think she'd take my threat lying down.

Flynn comes flying into the conference room, my harried assistant behind him, trying to stop his intrusion. He sends our mother an absolutely killing glare, then rushes to my side.

"This is all over the news. And if I've seen it, I guarantee Eryn has, too."

My brother shoves his phone in my face. A picture is worth a thousand words, but the caption makes everything seem even more damning.

WESTON SLEEPING HIS WAY TO THE TOP?

"That isn't me," I protest instantly.

"Nope."

Immediately, I understand. It's Edward. I don't know who captured this image or how, but I have zero doubt who leaked it to the press. And I swear I will throttle my mother—later.

All that matters now is getting to Eryn.

"Excuse me. I have an emergency I need to take care of."

Because if I don't explain these pictures to my fiancée right away, she'll leave me for good without ever hearing my explanation. And the man in this photo looks so much like me that I can hardly blame her.

My mother stands. "No, you'll stay. You have a presentation to give. The board has to vote."

I glance at my brother, and he nods.

"I'll stand in as his proxy and finish the presentation on his behalf."

"But you could lose the vote if you walk out!" my mother shrieks.

"Maybe. But that's not what's most important right now, and before you organized this debacle, you should have realized I'd say that."

"I'll call you later," Flynn assures me.

"Thanks, man. I owe you." I nod at the rest of the board. "My leaving is in no way indicative of how seriously I take this company and my position as CEO. Rest assured, only the most serious of incidents could induce me to leave now. Ms. Martin," I address Olivia. "I hope we can agree that you and I have never done more together than shake hands."

"We haven't. What's happening?" Then she reaches for

her phone, gasps, turns sheet-white and blinks up at me. "Oh, my god. No. This isn't you. I don't know how..."

I cut a glance at my mother that promises retribution. "I do." Then I turn to the board member most likely to oppose me. "Mr. Warren, you've always thought I lack the experience and wisdom necessary to do this job. Unlike my uncle, I have more integrity than to seduce or court your daughter simply to win your vote here today. If I get it, I hope that you voted for me because you respect me—at least more than someone capable of wooing a fellow board member and showing up for the vote after consuming half a bottle of vodka. But I've said my piece, and that's up to you. I leave the rest of this in everyone's hands." Then I turn to Flynn with a clap on the shoulder. "And yours. Thanks, bro."

After I walk out, ignoring my mother's gaping protests, I find a throng of tabloid bottom-feeders in the parking lot, waiting to take my statement. "I'm not the man in those pictures, and I have no other comment."

Why say more when they won't listen or believe me? Besides, only Eryn's opinion counts.

The drive back to the penthouse is a blur of multiple traffic violations. I screech to a halt in the parking garage and sprint all the way inside the building. I'm both rehearsing what I'm going to say to Eryn and cursing the slow elevator. My heart pounds. If I can't say or do the right things now, I will lose the woman I love—whom I will always love—and any chance of our happiness will be over.

Yes, I wish she simply believed me, but I know the disappointments in Eryn's life have been many, and that for years I was at the top of that list.

Finally, the elevator dings, and I step off.

I don't have to search for her. She's standing there, waiting for me, packed suitcases beside her. Her sisters and their men melt away, giving us blessed privacy.

"Eryn..." I shake my head. "Honey, it's not me in those pictures."

"How many times do you expect me to just believe you?" Tears fill her eyes. "You swore to me the other night that you weren't with Olivia Martin. I tried so hard to trust that you were telling me the truth. I was trying to put all my qualms aside and marry you anyway because what do we have without commitment and trust, right? Then these pictures surface. I know you needed her vote, but—"

"It's. Not. Me. I would never fuck someone for their support. More importantly, I would never do this to you." I rake my hand through my hair. "Hell, I walked out on the vote to reassure you. If jeopardizing my position as CEO isn't enough for you to believe that I will put you above all things—and that I wouldn't fuck someone to keep my title—then I don't know what else I can do. I see your bag is packed." I glance at her ring finger. It's bare, and I spot the box on the kitchen counter to her left. "And I guess you've made up your mind to let my mother win again. The first mistake was mine, and I take full responsibility for that. The second one, honey... This will be all on you. I can't be the only one fighting for us anymore. I'm still going to hope that you'll think about this overnight and want to marry me tomorrow. But if you don't"—I shrug—"I hate to sound cliché, but we'll both spend our lives miserable. And I'm such a stupid bastard. Because even if you walk out on me, I'm always going to love you."

CHAPTER ELEVEN

ERYN

I spend a miserable night with Señor Cuervo and my sisters in an unfamiliar but surprisingly posh hotel suite. Now, with the cold morning light filtering through the windows, my booze-and-tears hangover is killing my head. Despair weighs heavy on my heart.

Today is supposed to be my wedding day. But after yesterday's revelations...what the hell am I going to do?

"Morning," Ella murmurs.

I roll over. My older sister stands over me, holding a bottle of water and two ibuprofen. The concern on her face is sweet, but I don't need it half as much as I need those pills.

"Hey. Thanks." I grab the *agua* and the headache tablets, downing both.

"Did you sleep?"

"Enough. You okay?" I glance around the room. "Where's Echo?"

"With Hayes. I'm not entirely sure where they went."

Knowing Echo, she's hungry and wanted to find coffee that's organic, fair-trade, and piping hot.

"What about Carson?" I sit up and draw my knees to my chest.

She hesitates. "In our room, talking to West. Predictably, your fiancé wants to know if you're all right and if you'll be at the wedding."

Great question.

Last night proved that wallowing sucks, and drowning my insecurities with booze isn't effective, either.

The truth is, I need to get off my ass and decide what I want more—to avoid any possible chance of heartbreak or marriage to a man I love for however long he makes me happy.

"Can I ask you something?" I peer up at Ella. "I know you've only been married for two months, but you spoke your vows when you weren't totally sure. How has it been?"

"Fantastic. But that's us. Carson and I are dedicated to making our marriage work. Any relationship will fail unless both parties are committed to each other and resolving their conflicts. But if you can agree on that, you can overcome almost any obstacle. Do you love West?"

"Yes."

"Do you think he loves you?"

"In his way."

Ella frowns. "What way is that? He pursued you. He proposed to you twice. I overheard him on the phone late the other night, and he threatened his mother for you. He left the most important board meeting of his life—without any assurance he would remain CEO—for you. *All* for you. I know the circumstantial evidence looks bad, but...who are you going to believe? The man who's trying so hard to prove he loves you or his petty, controlling mother?"

My sister has a point—a damn good one, in fact. Would

West really have made any of those choices if he was willing to do *anything* to get ahead in business?

"Do you know what happened with yesterday's vote?"

"I don't." She winces. "West didn't say...and I don't think he cares about anything right now except you."

I close my eyes. "I've been a twit, haven't I? I let Miriam get in my head, even after he warned me. She knew exactly what to say, and I fell for it. Ugh. I feel stupid. Of course marriage doesn't come with guarantees."

"It doesn't."

I peek at Ella and find a curl playing at the corners of her lips.

"And I've been looking for one."

"More or less."

"I really have been a total twit."

"Pretty much."

Despite the grim situation, I laugh. "Thanks for sparing my feelings."

"What are sisters for?" Ella grins. "So...decision made?"

"Yeah. If West and I are going to fall apart, I refuse to let it be because I was too scared to commit or didn't give us my all. If we divorce someday, it will be on him. Because I'm going to do my best to be happy with the man I love."

Ella fakes a sniffle and wipes away a nonexistent tear. "I feel like such a proud mommy."

"Shut up. What time is it?"

"A little after eight."

"Shit. My hair appointment is in an hour. If I'm going to look like a bride, I have to get moving. Um, West still wants to get married today, right?"

"As of ten minutes ago, yes."

I bound out of bed, brush my teeth, and shove my hair into a ponytail. My head protests, but the rest of me is damn happy. It's my wedding day, and no one is going to steal my joy, least of all bitchy Miriam Quaid.

I've barely managed to toss on some clothes when I hear a knock at the door.

My sister and I share a glance. If it were Echo or Hayes, they'd either call out to us or let themselves in with a key. So who is it? Room service? Housekeeping?

Carson emerges from another bedroom with his phone pressed to his ear. "Yes, West. She's awake now. Let me ask..."

Ella gives Carson a thumbs-up and a grin. I nod at my brother-in-law in confirmation.

"And it looks like there will be a wedding today, buddy," Carson whoops into the phone. "Put on your tux."

Grinning, I head to the door and yank it open. I'm utterly shocked to see Edward Quaid standing at the threshold, looking contrite.

"What are you doing here?"

"Can I come in? I'd like to talk to you."

"I don't think we have anything to say, especially if you're going to proposition me again."

He winces. "Did I do that? I'm sorry. I'd had too much to drink. I often...overcompensate with liquid fortification when I know I have to face Miriam and West. I just want five minutes of your time."

With a sigh, I step back and let him in. He eases past me,

heading for the desk chair.

I sit on the edge of the bed, facing him, appreciating the way my sister melts into the background. Carson drifts to a corner, watching protectively.

"You need help," I tell Edward.

"I know. Yesterday, I had the worst day of my life. And yet, I'm wondering if it was all for the best." He sighs. "I lost the vote."

I'm relieved for West's sake, yet oddly sad for this man. "I'm sorry. I know you wanted to run Quaid Enterprises."

"I did. Or I thought I did. But I never really questioned why. Tradition? Expectation?" He shrugs. "But losing yesterday helped me to put that part of my life behind me so I can move forward."

"Great. So you'll go on serving on Quaid's board and doing...whatever else it is you do. And have more time for treatment and counseling." And I'm happy for him, but I wonder why Edward is here, telling *me* all this.

"Not exactly. You didn't hear?"

I shake my head. "What?"

"Well, West retains his position as CEO, of course."

That will make my fiancé happy. He runs the company so well, like he was born to do it. "And?"

"Those shadowy pictures that appear to be of West and Olivia Martin?" He shakes his head. "I'm the man in those images with her."

A gasp slips from my throat. The profile looked so much like West... I might have suspected Flynn of seducing the young widow. Edward never crossed my mind. "Oh, my god."

"The affair had been going on for a few weeks."

So it really wasn't West trolling for votes and shitting all over the commitment we made to each other. My head wanted to believe that all along, but my heart is so relieved for the proof.

Guilt follows. I should have trusted my husband-to-be. I should never have listened to his poisonous mother.

I never will again.

Edward sighs. "The board found out I'd been...um, doing favors, opening doors, and offering cash to some of the others in exchange for their vote. They ousted me. So, no more Quaid Enterprises. No more worrying or fixating on the company I grew up thinking I'd always have a hand in. I'm still part owner since it's a family business. I'll get to share in the profits, but I'm no longer allowed to dabble in anything operational. And my wife saw my salacious images with Olivia, realized I was the man in the picture, and left me last night. She isn't coming back."

Holy crap, he really did have a terrible day. I don't like this man when he's drunk, but weirdly he seems all right sober.

I place my hand over his. "I'm sorry."

"Thanks. But actually...I'm not. Normally, yesterday would have sent me straight for a bottle. But suddenly, I was stone sober, and I realized that for the first time in forever, I had nothing to drink away. At forty-three, I have a clean slate in life. I can move on to other responsibilities and healthier relationships. For once, I can choose what makes me happy—my job, my significant other. Everything. The lifelong expectations that come with being a Quaid heir? Gone. I'm looking forward to starting over. But the first thing I wanted to do was tell you that West never touched Olivia. My nephew loves you desperately. I'm hardly an expert on love since I'm clearly going to be divorced soon, but you should marry him."

When he stands, I smile. "I'm going to. Thanks for coming to explain. It's really decent of you."

He shoots me a self-deprecating grin. "I haven't been accused of that in the last couple of decades, but I'm going to do better. There's a great health and wellness spa in Tucson. I'm going to spend two weeks at Miraval, then I think I'll relocate somewhere quieter. Somewhere I don't have to be reminded of the past. I've always wanted to live in Montana. Who knows?"

"Do what makes you happy. Just don't be a total stranger, huh?"

Somehow, I think West and I might miss an Edward full of peace and calm.

"You got it." He heads for the door. "Oh, want to hear maybe the best part of the board meeting?"

Besides West getting to keep his job? "Please."

"On my way out, I told everyone that Miriam had leaked the pictures to the press. I have to give her credit. Her ploy was brilliant, really. She released the images of Olivia and me, insisting it was West. She suspected you would take the story at face value and leave her son for good. But she also knew the board would demand proof since the seduction clearly took place on Quaid's premises. Sure enough, they pulled up the security footage, realized it was me, and ousted me for tampering with the vote. Two birds, one stone. But it backfired. The security officer she bribed for the footage

MISADVENTURES WITH MY EX

valued staying out of jail more than he valued the ten thousand Miriam gave him. Apparently, he sang like a canary. So..." His grin widens. "Miriam is no longer on the board, either. In fact, she's forbidden from being involved in any way with Quaid again, except cashing the checks that come with being Kingston's widow. Sometimes justice is sweet."

A wide smile peels across my face. "Really? The cow is gone?"

"Oh, yeah. And I imagine after her latest stunt, West will have almost nothing to do with his mother again."

Maybe. Maybe not. I'll leave that up to him. But the good news is, she lost. And unless we let her, she can't touch us again.

Impulsively, I hug Edward. "Thanks again. Seriously, good luck with everything."

"You're welcome. Be sure to live happily ever after for me, will you?"

"Absolutely. I plan to start today."

WEST

Tension gnawing at my stomach, I glance at my watch. Five minutes until one.

At the altar, I turn to look at Flynn. "You're sure Eryn is here?"

My brother sends me an indulgent smile. "Positive. She looks beautiful, too."

Of course she does; that's a given. "She's going to walk down the aisle in five minutes?"

"Yes."

"Chill, buddy," Carson says beside Flynn, standing in for

my other groomsman, a high school pal who sadly contracted the flu. "She'll be here. And pretty soon, you'll know what a roller coaster it is to be married to one of the Hope sisters. Good luck!"

Hayes laughs from the front row. "I can only imagine. This is when I'm glad to just be Echo's friend."

Carson and I exchange a glance. Yeah, neither of us think the platonic thing between those two makes sense...or will last much longer.

Instead, Ella's husband drawls, "They can be hell on wheels. But they can also be the warmest, most amazing women on the planet. You got a keeper."

"I know." It's one reason I'm so desperate to marry Eryn. The other reason? I'm pretty sure my life will never be complete without her.

The moments drag on until the ordained minister, whom we had to request *not* be dressed as Elvis, files in from the back of the building. His assistant, dressed in a skimpy, glittery uniform, skips out to check the flower arrangements, grab a camera, then retreat to a corner of the sanctuary, pressing a button to start the music along the way.

A sweeping instrumental ballad fills the air. Echo walks down the aisle in a long dress that's a soft blend of beige and pink. The strapless gown hangs in a long sweep to her bare feet, unbroken except for an expanse of lace that begins just above her breasts and hangs nearly to her tiny waist. She's also wearing a crown of flowers in her loosely braided hair and a smile.

I glance at Hayes. He looks unblinking and dumbstruck.

I wonder what the odds are that they'll be "just friends" after tonight...

Then Ella files in behind Echo, wearing the same color in a simple wrap-front style that cascades down to her stylish shoes and shows off her petite curves. Carson looks both proud and sincerely in love.

When she reaches the altar, the music changes. The doors at the back of the chapel open.

And there stands Eryn, in her wedding dress with her veil swathing her narrow torso, wearing a bright smile. Confidence and happiness shine from her eyes.

I lose my breath. God, she's so gorgeous. And about to be all mine...

The best part? One glance, and I know she has no reservations about marrying me. She's ready for this. For us. For forever. We're going to be happy.

The only people attending our wedding on my side of the chapel are Gen, Flynn, and a handful of loyal Quaid board members. Today, more than ever, I miss my grandfather. But he's here with me in spirit. I've chosen well, followed my heart. I can feel his approval.

Now, all I have left to do is slide a ring on Eryn's finger so we can start living what I'm sure will be an interesting, passionate, sometimes chaotic, mostly sublime life.

I lean closer to the officiant. "Can we, um...speed this up? I'm really impatient to be married to this woman."

He slants a glance at me, brow raised. "How fast?"

"If you can finish this in less than ten minutes, there's an extra grand in it for you."

"Done."

That makes me smile. I hope Eryn doesn't mind that I'm rushing our ceremony. I'd rather get on with all our shared tomorrows. We still have to figure out where we'll live and what she's going to do with her restaurant. But that's geography. One of us will move, and that's that. I refuse to let location be an obstacle, and given the resolve on my bride's face, I'm pretty sure she feels the same.

It seems to take forever for Eryn to reach me. It's probably twenty seconds; the place isn't huge. But it's nineteen seconds too long.

Finally, she's beside me, and I'm pulling her close for a lingering kiss.

"We're not to that part of the ceremony, Mr. Quaid," the officiant murmurs.

The crowd twitters.

I can't help but smile. "Give me a minute."

With the music swelling in the background, I cup my bride's shoulders. "Eryn—"

"I'm sorry," she blurts. "I love you. I trust you. I want to spend my life with you."

My heart swells. "I love you, too, honey. So much. You want to get married now?"

She nods, then glances at the officiant. "I do."

"We're not to that part of the ceremony, either," the robed man drawls, drawing more laughter from the crowd.

"Can we...you know, hurry this along?"

I burst out laughing. This woman really is perfect for me.

"I moonlight as an auctioneer. I can make this go really

fast, if you want."

Eryn glances at me. I peer back. Wearing conspiratorial grins, we nod.

He rolls through the welcome, introduction, and "marriage is" speech in less than three minutes, sounding all the while like he's selling someone's valuables, but I don't care. I don't want to waste another moment of my life without this woman, and I don't want to let another tick of the clock slide by without calling her my wife.

Finally, we come to the part of the ceremony where we exchange vows. Not-Elvis recites them so fast, I can barely understand what I'm supposed to repeat. I do my best, flubbing a lot, I'm sure. Eryn and I both laugh. Then she does the same, and it's somehow even funnier, sweeter. Barely six minutes into the ceremony, we're sliding rings on each other's fingers and the officiant is pronouncing us man and wife.

Finally.

I kiss my bride with all the passion and longing I've stored up while wondering if she would ever truly be mine. Hell, if I would ever even see her again. She kisses me back with love and penitence and so much gusto, I wonder how we're going to manage the short reception and even shorter ride to the honeymoon suite I booked. Thankfully, I'm going to surprise her with a week in Maui at the most amazing little bed-and-breakfast.

It's the perfect way to start our married life together—naked, together, joined, and committed.

Carson clears his throat a long moment later, and we come up for air. The onlookers are now laughing outright as we clasp hands and run back down the aisle.

We grudgingly pause in the vestibule to pose for pictures taken by the chapel assistant.

The minister approaches. "This is one of the most interesting weddings I've ever officiated. And in this town, that's saying something." He sticks out his hand. "Congratulations, Mr. and Mrs. Quaid."

"Thanks." I slip him the extra bills promised and watch him disappear with a smile. Then I turn to my wife. Wow, it feels good to say that.

The reception seems to last five years. I shake the hands of all the well-wishers who came to our wedding. Eryn and I drink champagne, eat cake, and kiss as if we're making a promise each time our lips meet.

"Do you forgive me?" my wife asks as we dance.

I caress her cheek. "Of course. I know Mom. I know how persuasive she can be and how deadly accurate her barbs are. I should have been there for you."

"The elevator really broke down?"

"Yes. I was so pissed. And so worried about you."

"I heard the board meeting went well."

He grins. "Couldn't have asked for better. The vote to keep me as CEO was almost unanimous. Best of all, Uncle Eddie and Mom are both out of my hair."

"I'm thrilled about your mother, but Edward... He came to see me this morning. When he's not drunk, he's actually a good guy."

I shrug. "I haven't seen him sober in years, so maybe you're right. But what's best about yesterday's meeting is that Flynn and Gen were voted into their vacant seats, so now I'll never have to worry about enduring a no-confidence vote again. I'm going to run Quaid Enterprises for a long time."

"And you'll do a great job. I'm going to be by your side... after I finish college."

"You've decided to go back to school?"

"I'd like to. Is that okay? I hear UNLV has a pretty good program for hospitality management."

"What about Java and Jacks?"

"Believe it or not, I got a call about two hours ago from the owner of the tchotchke shop next door. They want to expand their space and asked if there was any way I'd be willing to sell out. We came to terms...so I'm not a restaurant owner anymore. But I will be again someday."

Damn, this day could not have turned out more perfect. "I know you will, and Vegas will be a great place to open whatever you want."

"Exactly. But first, I seriously need to tear apart that penthouse of yours and make it look less like Wayne Newton's love shack and more like a home for us."

"Do whatever you want, wife...as long as you're totally available to me every night. Six p.m. to six a.m."

"Oh, you're not just stuck with me twelve hours a day. I'll be here twenty-four seven. For the rest of your life."

She leans in to kiss me, and I savor the meshing of our mouths, of our lives. The music plays on, and I hold her tight.

When the song ends, we finally come up for air. Everyone claps, and I don't know if that's because we danced or made out through most of the song. Who cares?

I've got Eryn, so I've got the world.

"How much longer do you think we have to be polite and mingle with everyone?" she murmurs in my ear, sounding breathy.

I glance at my watch. "We've been here seventy-two minutes. That's long enough, right?"

"Totally."

"Where's the honeymoon suite?"

"Not far. The question you should be asking me is where's the honeymoon itself?"

Her eyes widen. "You're serious? We're going somewhere?"

My grin turns seductive when I think of all the long days and nights alone with my new bride. "Baldwin Beach. For a week."

"Where's that?"

"It's a surprise. But you know what I heard from this really gorgeous—albeit drunk—woman not long ago, wearing a dress that looks surprisingly like this one?"

Eryn giggles. "Do tell..."

"All the best beaches start with a B. Ready to find out if that's true?"

Laughing, she tosses herself against me. "And you'll be with me at this beach?"

"Yes."

"Will the orgasm quotient be high?"

"Not just high, but so massive it will be disgusting. You're going to come home with noodle legs and a really loopy smile, Mrs. Quaid."

"You too." She tugs on my hand and leads me toward the door. "Let's go."

I sling an arm around her waist and follow. "You know I never stopped loving you."

She pauses and kisses me softly. "I never stopped, either. And now we've got each other for the rest of our lives."

MORE MISADVENTURES

ALSO FROM SHAYLA BLACK

More Than Need You

Meet Griffin Reed. He discovered his ex's secret. Now, he's willing to do anything to win her back in MORE THAN NEED YOU, part of Shayla's steamy, emotional More Than Words series.

Keep reading for an excerpt!

MORE THAN NEED YOU

More Than Words: Book Two

I'm Griffin Reed—cutthroat entrepreneur and competitive bastard. Trust is a four-letter word and everyone is disposable...except Britta Stone. Three years ago, she was my everything before I stupidly threw her away. I thought I'd paid for my sin in misery—until I learned we have a son. Finding out she's engaged to a bore who's rushing her to the altar pisses me off even more. I intend to win her back and raise our boy. I'll have to get ruthless, of course. Luckily, that's one of my most singular talents.

Sixty days. That's what I'm asking the gritty, independent single mother to give me—twenty-four/seven. Under my roof. And if I have my way, in my bed. Britta says she wants nothing to do with me. But her body language and passionate kisses make her a liar. Now all I have to do is coax her into surrendering to the old magic between us. Once I have her right where I want her, I'll do whatever it takes to prove I more than need her.

★ ★ ★

"Take this." She lifts the first chair and proffers it to me, holding it between us.

I take it from her grasp. "Got it."

The tension between us is a tingle prickling the back of my neck.

"Thanks." Her hands are shaking. Her gaze won't quite meet mine.

She's visibly nervous. Because I make her feel something. Maxon swears she's still in love with me. If I want Britta back, I need to tell her how I feel. It's something I've historically sucked at. I also have to give her a reason to open up to me in return.

This is my moment. My heart is thudding manically. Maxon stayed in the living/dining room. Jamie is surely sleeping in his crib. And we're not in the office. This chance alone with her may not come around again soon. All I have to do is kick the bedroom door shut behind me.

Anxiety nearly chokes me. But if I'm ever going to win her back, I can't give Britta less than my all now.

I set the chair aside and grab her hand. "I'm not the same man I used to be, I swear."

She searches my face. "Let go."

If I do what she asks, I'll only give her time to build a taller wall between us before I've even begun chipping away at the one she's already got in place.

I cup her hand tighter. "I was a bastard. Three years ago, I didn't value you the way I should have. I didn't love you the way I meant to. I..." Finding the right words is harder than I imagined. "I never meant to hurt you. But I know I did."

She's had a long time to lovingly craft creative curses to rain on my head for the shit I did to her. I'm expecting to hear a litany of them. Instead, hurt flashes in her eyes. "What do you want me to say, Griff? What are you looking for? Absolution?"

"Be mad. Yell at me. It's okay. I'll answer your questions. I'll stand here and take your anger. Whatever will prove I'm serious. Whatever you need to feel better."

"I don't feel anything at all." She wriggles free and turns to retrieve another chair.

Liar.

So she doesn't want to talk? Well, some situations call for more than words. They've never been my strong suit anyway.

I take the second chair from her grip and set it in the corner beside the first. Then I wrap my fingers around her elbow and give a gentle tug. She stumbles against me. Our chests collide. She gasps. Her head snaps back. I pull her body closer to mine. Our eyes meet.

"Angel," I whisper as I cradle her cheeks in my hands and drop my head. She barely has time to draw another breath before I settle my lips over hers.

Then I'm kissing Britta again after three long fucking years.

A million sensations hit me at once. I inhale her familiar jasmine scent. I caress the velvet of her face, her nape. I hear her rapid intake of breath. Heat burns my veins. I'm melting. Her touch feels so electric. I'm dying. Holding her again is so stunning. Arousal hammers me—heart pinging, breaths sawing, cock hardening. But my feelings aren't the same as before. Now they're desperate. They're so yearning. So deep.

They're the feelings of a man who finally understands love—and has been given a second chance to give it back.

Touching her is also a comfort, like coming home after

a long war. I feel as if I've fought myself and exorcised the demons of my past. I'm unshackled but I'm so chained to her that I'll never be free. I don't want to be.

Memories of the hundreds of times I stripped her bare, physically and sexually, and left her blushing and smiling and panting my name bombard me. I'm haunted by the times she told me she loved me and I said nothing in return.

Against me she's frozen in shock. Her body is tense. Her fingers are splayed wide on my chest where they landed when she tried to catch her balance. She's not moving her lips against mine. And goddamn it, I crave her response. I have to know I'm not the only one willing to give us another try.

With a groan, I brush my lips over Britta's again. If anything, she goes stiffer. I breathe against her and try like hell to coax her. I almost back off. But...she's not yelling at me. She's not shoving me away.

I try one more time, giving her a suede-soft slide of my lips over hers. Then suddenly, she trembles under me. Her fingers begin to curl into my shirt. I sense that she wants to give in...but is trying so hard not to.

"Kiss me." I nudge her mouth open and hover. "Just once. I've missed you like hell."

The still moment hangs, suspended. Then finally she exhales and closes her eyes. Her arms curl around my neck. A little moan escapes the back of her throat as she tilts her head, parts her lips for me...

And she invites me in.

With a low groan, I fuse our mouths together and taste

that something sweet, elusive, and addictive that's purely Britta. She softens against me and pours herself into our kiss. Every breath, every crush of lips, every slide of tongue—she's with me. She curls her fingers into fists, grabbing my shirt before she uses it to drag me closer. But there's already no air between us.

Emboldened, I dive deeper inside her. One kiss bleeds into the next, endless and urgent. Right now, I don't give a shit if we ever come up for air.

With seeking palms, I slide my way down the bare skin of her waist until I'm gripping her hips and grinding her pussy against my aching cock. Tingles ignite and explode, and I groan into her mouth. I want her to know how much she affects me. She should never again feel less than confident about how desperately I want her. I also realize one other undeniable fact.

I. Am. Hers.

My hands slide down from her hips to cup her pert backside. In one grunt, I lift her against me, spread her thighs around my hips, and rock against her. She turns frantic, eating at my mouth, pulling at my hair, like she's looking for some way to be closer, let me deeper inside. She climbs my body and wraps her legs around me, trying to wriggle against me for friction.

My heart is racing so fast I swear it's going to explode. And I don't care. I keep at her. The only thing that will stop me now is if she says no. And the way our chemistry feels... I'm not sure that word is in her vocabulary anymore.

Holy fuck. This is hotter than anything I've ever felt.

I break away from the kiss to look at her. But I can't stand any distance between us. I brush my lips over her neck. My teeth nip at her lobe. I breathe across her skin. She shivers, opening her eyes just enough to reveal her heavy lids and dilated pupils.

"Griff..." She tilts her head back and shifts restlessly over my erection again with a groan.

Continue Reading in More Than Need You!

CONNECT WITH
SHAYLA BLACK

Let's get to know each other!

Connect with me via the links below. The VIP Readers newsletter has exclusive news and excerpts. You can also become one of my Facebook Book Beauties and enjoy live #WineWednesday video chats full of fun, book chatter, and more! See you soon!

Website: ShaylaBlack.com

VIP Reader Newsletter: Shayla.link/nwsltr

Facebook: Facebook.com/ShaylaBlackAuthor

Facebook Book Beauties Chat Group:
Shayla.link/FBChat

Instagram: Instagram.com/ShaylaBlack

Twitter: Twitter.com/Shayla_Black

Amazon Author: Shayla.link/AmazonFollow

BookBub: Shayla.link/BookBub

Goodreads: Shayla.link/GoodReads

YouTube: Shayla.link/YouTube

ALSO BY SHAYLA BLACK

His to Take
Pure Wicked: Novella
Wicked for You
Falling in Deeper
Dirty Wicked: Novella
A Very Wicked Christmas: Short
Holding on Tighter

The Devoted Lovers
Devoted to Pleasure (Coming Soon)
Devoted to Wicked: Novella
Devoted to Love (July 2, 2019)

Sexy Capers
Bound and Determined
Strip Search
Arresting Desire: Hot in Handcuffs Anthology

The Perfect Gentlemen
(by Shayla Black and Lexi Blake)
Scandal Never Sleeps
Seduction in Session
Big Easy Temptation
Smoke and Sin
At the Pleasure of the President (Spring 2019)

Masters of Ménage
(by Shayla Black and Lexi Blake)
Their Virgin Captive

Their Virgin's Secret
Their Virgin Concubine
Their Virgin Princess
Their Virgin Hostage
Their Virgin Secretary
Their Virgin Mistress
Their Virgin Bride (Coming Soon)

Doms of Her Life
(by Shayla Black, Jenna Jacob, and Isabella LaPearl)
The Complete Raine Falling Collection
One Dom to Love
The Young and the Submissive
The Bold and the Dominant
The Edge of Dominance

Heavenly Rising Collection
The Choice
The Chase (2019)

The Misadventures Series
Misadventures of a Backup Bride
Misadventures with My Ex

<u>Standalone Titles</u>

Naughty Little Secret
Watch Me
Dangerous Boys and Their Toy

Her Fantasy Men: Four Play Anthology
A Perfect Match
His Forbidden Secret: Sexy Short

Historical Romance

(as Shelley Bradley)
The Lady and the Dragon
One Wicked Night
Strictly Seduction
Strictly Forbidden

Brothers in Arms: Medieval Trilogy
His Lady Bride (Book 1)
His Stolen Bride (Book 2)
His Rebel Bride (Book 3)

Paranormal Romance

The Doomsday Brethren
Tempt Me with Darkness
Fated: e-Novella
Seduce Me in Shadow
Possess Me at Midnight
Mated: Haunted by Your Touch Anthology
Entice Me at Twilight
Embrace Me at Dawn

Find all of these titles at ShaylaBlack.com!